From the Heart

Heart

Book Two The McBrides

Jax Burrows

Jax Burrows

Manchester

M18 7HN

United Kingdom

https://www.jburrowsauthor.com

Book Layout © 2023 Atticus

Cover Design by James T Egan https://www.bookflydesign.com/

Contents

CHAPTER ONE

'Wow!' said Noah Whittaker as he looked around Candy McBride's living-room. 'It's very green. Is this a Saint Patrick's Day party, or are we celebrating Scarlett's birthday?'

'Both. It was a joke that became a tradition,' said Esme McBride, his soon-to-be sister-in-law who had started helping her mum as soon as she'd taken her coat off. 'Scarlett's still upstairs getting ready by the way.'

How quickly things could change. Before his younger brother, Joel, fell in love with Esme, the eldest of the McBride sisters, the only contact Noah had had with Scarlett had been at work. He liked the sparky redhead, they worked well together and he admired her skills as a mental health nurse. But he had known little about her private life. Now, he was in the thick of things, helping her celebrate her thirty-first birthday.

Noah wasn't totally sure how he felt about it, not being a very sociable person. He preferred his own company to parties, but now he was here, he intended to make the most of it and help Scarlett celebrate in style.

The house had been decorated with tiny leprechauns and sham-rocks as well as Happy Birthday banners, Happy Saint Patrick's Day banners, and green streamers and balloons. There were even green napkins and runners on the table which was laden with food including a marvellous bright green birthday cake. There was also plenty of booze; wine, beer, and champagne. And soft drinks, he noted.

'Go on,' said Noah, 'tell us this story.' Now he was almost part of the family, he was interested to know more about them.

'You tell it, Mum,' said Esme to Candy.

'You couldn't stick the kettle on, could you? I'll have champagne later when we toast the birthday girl, but I could murder a cuppa now,' said Dot, Candy's business partner, who was red in the face from all the walking from the kitchen to the dining-room with plates and dishes.

'I can do that if you're all busy,' Noah offered.

'No, no, we've got everything covered,' Candy assured him.

'I'll make it,' said Maria the second-youngest McBride sister.

So Noah stood in the kitchen doorway watching the women scurry around like worker ants on a deadline. He hoped if he waited long enough someone would get around to telling the story.

'What would you like to drink, Noah?' asked Candy, 'We have Guinness?'

'I'll have a soft drink please. Lemonade will do.'

'Coming up. Anyway, Saint Patrick's Day. When Scarlett was a teenager she was a bit of a rebel and decided not to celebrate her birthday.'

'What, Scarlett a rebel? Never.' Noah chuckled.

'Hey, I heard that.' He turned around then stopped in his tracks. She was dressed all in green; a tight green dress, green tights, green shoes, and a hat with shamrocks and A Happy Saint Patrick's Day on a band around it. With her red hair, she looked a picture. 'Ta da! What do you think? Green enough?'

Noah dropped a kiss on her cheek, and for a split second, he wished he could have kissed her mouth. Where had that idea come from? He'd never wanted to kiss her before. He shook the thought away putting it down to the fact they were at a party and she looked amazing in her costume. Their gaze held and Noah's breath quickened. 'You're missing the green wig and lipstick,' he murmured. Then, to bring things back to the level of the platonic he asked, 'So, how old were you when you decided not to celebrate your birthday?'

'Thirteen,' she replied moving away from him to the table laden with food. 'I thought it was uncool to still be having birthday parties like a little kid.' She selected a sausage roll and took a bite.

'Her dad and me wouldn't let an important birthday pass uncelebrated so we took Scarlett and a few of her closest friends out for a meal. It was a very serious affair as the only meal they'd had out up to then had been burger and chips.' Candy steered her daughter gently away from the table.

'I thought that was it, but of course Mum and Dad had other ideas.' Scarlett grinned and Noah couldn't take his eyes off her.

'We decided to have a party but call it a Saint Patrick's Day party. We had Gaelic music, folk dancing on the lawn and even Guinness although I don't think anyone drank it.'

'I did,' said Dot, as she carried more dishes from the kitchen to the dining room. 'It's a good source of iron.'

'I don't remember that,' said Connie the youngest McBride. She had wandered in from the garden, apparently tired of throwing a tennis ball for Crazy Boy, Dot's highly strung collie cross.

Noah watched the activity of the McBride family. It reminded him of a beehive, with the workers buzzing around busily. Candy was queen bee of course.

'You were only three, you can't possibly remember it,' Scarlett said. The doorbell rang. 'I'll get it.'

A moment later Noah heard an excited squeal from the hallway. 'You're here! It's so good to see you both.'

Scarlett came back into the living-room with two women who carried presents and bottles of wine.

Noah had never attended a party with so many women and only two men. He wasn't great at socialising, preferring his own company, but put on a smile to join the family in greeting the newcomers.

'Everyone—this is Sadie and Megs. You know my family and Dot, but you haven't met the Whittaker brothers. This is Joel who's engaged to Esme, and this is Noah his brother who I also happen to work with.'

'Congratulations, Esme! When's the wedding?' asked Megs who was small, dark, and pretty.

'May,' said Esme with a beaming smile.

'I'm chief bridesmaid and Noah is best man,' said Scarlett.

Both girls turned their attention to Noah. Megs looked him up and down as if he was on sale in a market. She obviously liked what she saw as she fluttered her eyelashes and gave him a come-to-bed look. Sadie, who was plump and rather plain, blushed.

'Pleased to meet you, ladies,' he said. He felt uncomfortable under Megs' scrutiny. His smile of greeting slipped slightly as she continued her inspection of him. His stomach clenched, but fortunately, Scarlett dragged her into a group hug with Sadie. He watched the three of them who'd been friends since university jumping up and down together like little girls in a playground. He'd lost touch with all his friends from his medical student days. He didn't want to be reminded of the person he was then.

'Are we all here? Not waiting for anyone else, Scarlett?' asked Candy who was in her element with a house full of people. She looked beautiful in a long, colourful summer dress, and smoky eye make-up, like a femme fatale.

'No, Mum, everyone's here.'

Scarlett turned to him with a smile. 'Food. Are you hungry?'

'Now you mention it, I am. But before we eat, I've got you a gift.' Noah took a small box out of his pocket. He hadn't known what to get her and ended up asking Esme, and now he was strangely nervous. Was it an appropriate gift for someone he worked with? Was it too personal? Should he have just bought her some chocolates or something?

I haven't wrapped it, I hope that's okay.'

'Thanks, that's really kind of you. Scarlett took the box and opened it. She took out a silver heart on a chain and studied it carefully. Noah held his breath as he waited for her reaction. 'It's gorgeous!'

Thank goodness. She seemed genuinely pleased with it. 'Shall I put it on for you?' he asked.

'Yes, please.'

Scarlett lifted her hair so he could fasten the chain around her neck. He breathed in her perfume and the smell of apples from her hair. When his fingers brushed the back of her neck she shivered. Or maybe he imagined that.

He stepped away from her. 'There. I didn't put any pictures in it as I didn't know what you'd want.'

'I'll find something special to put in it. Maybe my mum and dad as they would have been celebrating their thirty-fifth wedding anniversary this year if Dad had lived.' Scarlett gazed into the middle distance and her eyes were misty. She fingered the necklace absent-mindedly.

'I'm sorry.' Noah couldn't help but think how inadequate those words were. But Candy saved him from having to think of anything more fitting to say to Scarlett.

'Right everyone,' Candy said, 'let's eat.'

A cheer went up and a queue formed at the dining table. Noah loaded his plate with pizza, chicken wings and rice salad, then looked around for somewhere to sit. There weren't many chairs, so he lounged against the wall instead. Joel joined him, his plate full to overflowing.

'Hungry?' Noah asked.

'Starving,' said Joel, biting into a piece of garlic bread.

'I wanted to check that the plans for the stag night still stand. Stay in Leytonsfield and have a few drinks?'

Joel nodded, swallowing before he answered. 'Yes. No meals, clubs, strippers, or any of that malarkey. Keep it simple, tasteful, and cheap. The wedding is expensive enough.' He shrugged and rolled his eyes.

'You're okay for money though?' Noah wouldn't let a little thing like filthy lucre prevent his baby brother having the best wedding he could.

'Yes, we're fine. Just being careful.' Joel grinned and Noah sensed Esme's influence in the decision.

Esme and Joel were paying for their own wedding as Candy couldn't afford it all. She insisted on paying for the dress.

'Okay. A simple, tasteful stag night. Got it. What's Esme planned for her hen night?'

'Uh… she hasn't said. I'm not sure she's even thought about it.'

'She'll have thought about it alright. Esme's the most organised person I've ever met. She won't leave anything to chance. So you'd better put your thinking cap on and come up with a list of people you want me to invite. Time's ticking on.' Noah bit into a slice of pizza. It was still hot and very tasty.

'Okay, I'll get onto it. There won't be many of us though. You and the men who work in the medical centre, plus some friends from Manchester.'

'It's your stag night, bro, whatever you want we'll do.' Noah was determined to play his part in making this wedding go with a bang and the stag night was the start of that.

'Right.' Joel had finished his enormous plate of food and looked longingly at the dining-table which was still laden with goodies. 'Are you going to risk that green cake?'

'I bet we'll have to sing Happy Birthday to Scarlett before we'll be allowed anywhere near that cake.'

'Okay. I'll go and see what else is on offer.'

Noah watched Joel chatting to people as he made his way to the table. How strange that his baby brother would be the first to be married. Not that Noah minded. In fact he was relieved. The thought of marriage brought him out in a rash. This way their parents would have their grandchildren, leaving him to do his own thing. But Joel had never been happier, and Noah was determined to help him make his wedding day the best day of his life.

CHAPTER TWO

S carlett didn't know whether to squirm with embarrassment or grin with pleasure, so she did both. All the people she cared about most were together singing Happy Birthday to her. It made her feel tearful, and a bit embarrassed as Noah was also singing. She wasn't entirely sure why that would be embarrassing, but it was.

'Thank you everyone and thank you for coming today, it means a lot.' She managed to hold back the tears at the sight of all the beloved faces beaming at her.

Her mum hugged her and kissed her on the cheek before murmuring, 'Happy Birthday, darling.'

'Thanks Mum, for everything.'

The rest of the family swooped in for their hugs.

Noah was watching on the side-lines, but he didn't approach until everyone else had done so. He ambled over and enveloped her in a bear hug. His closeness speeded up her heartrate and left her breathless. Her face was in his neck and some errant part of her brain wondered what he'd do if she kissed him there. She breathed in the mixed aromas of freshly showered man; shampoo, shower gel, something else that she couldn't identify. She'd call it Eau de Noah.

Why was she thinking like this? It wasn't as if she fancied him or anything. Did she? He was a work colleague that was all. Soon to be a brother-in-law.

'Happy Birthday, Scarlett, and thank you for asking me to your party.' He kissed her chastely on the cheek and she felt inexplicably let down.

'Thank you for coming and for the lovely present.' Despite the mundanity of their conversation Scarlett felt as if she didn't want to let go. It was a wonderful hug and she could have stayed like this all day.

She'd asked him to her party as he would soon be a member of her family. Despite working together, they hardly ever socialised. The Christmas party, an occasional drink in the nearest pub if a member of staff was leaving, but the rest of the time was strictly business. Then when Esme fell in love with Joel, Noah became so much more. She wanted him to feel welcome and part of things. She just hoped he wanted that too.

'Right, everyone,' said Candy, 'Raise your glasses please to wish Scarlett a happy birthday.'

Noah released her to raise his glass. A bit reluctantly, Scarlett thought.

Everyone shouted, 'Happy Birthday!' as loudly as they could.

'Now the candles,' said Connie, 'I hope you've got enough puff to blow them all out. Thirty-one candles, oh my!'

'Of course, let me at it.' Why did Connie always have to remind her of her age? She felt old enough without constant reminders from her baby sister.

There were only four candles, one for each decade and one extra. Scarlett half expected them to be the trick ones that never went out, but she blew them out easily.

The cake was a work of art in three layers of bright green sponge with white creamy icing and green and gold candles. Her mum would have worked hard at baking the best cake she could. Scarlett felt a lump in her throat at how much she did for them all. She'd never be able to repay her, however much she tried.

When the cake had been cut and served and there was nothing left on the plate but crumbs, Scarlett whistled loudly to get everyone's attention.

'Right,' she called, who's for dancing?'

What a great party. Good food, drink, her two besties here. All her family. She was determined to make the most of every second. Could she get Noah to dance with her? She looked over at him standing with his brother. They didn't look all that much alike. Joel was blonde with blue eyes, and Noah had dark brown hair with brown eyes.

'I've eaten too much,' groaned Joel.

'I never thought I'd ever hear that sentence from you, bro,' said Noah laughing.

The music was, of course, Irish folk music and the champagne was still flowing along with the wine and beer. Champagne Scarlett had been drinking as if it was lemonade. Maybe she should slow down. No! This was her birthday party and she was going to enjoy herself. Scarlett Irish-jigged herself over to her friends.

'Why are there so few men at this party?' asked Megs who was swaying gently and trying to focus.

'Sorry, Megs.' Scarlett wasn't really sorry; she was having a thoroughly good time. Anyway, she was used to being surrounded by women. 'But you seem to be enjoying yourself despite that. How about the three of us getting together one night for a good catch up?'

'Sounds good to me. Where's that good looking one got to?' Meg squinted and scrutinised the room.

'You mean Noah?' Who else could she mean? She knew Joel was engaged to Esme.

'Is he married?'

'Noah? No, not married.' She hoped Megs hadn't got Noah in her sights. She needed to put her off because… well, just because.

'Engaged? Spoken for? Gay?'

'No, none of those things. He's the consultant psychiatrist in the unit I work in and Joel's brother.'

'So he'll be your brother-in-law then?'

'Correct.' Scarlett didn't know how she felt about that yet.

'So, d'ya think I have a chance?' Megs grinned, looking hopeful.

'A chance for what?' Scarlett knew exactly what but played dumb hoping Megs would change the subject. They should have invited more men. Megs was an attractive woman and confident around men. She saw them as a challenge.

'A chance with the fair doctor of course. His brother's spoken for so…'

'It's not for me to say.' The conversation was sailing into dangerous waters. She had no intention of setting Meg up with Noah.

'Unless you want him for yourself, is that it?'

'No, of course not. What an idea. Preposterous.'

'Oopsy,' said Megs trying to point behind Scarlett, but obviously finding it hard to focus after having more than her share of the champagne.

Scarlett turned around. Noah was standing behind her and he must have heard every word. His expression was unreadable.

'Noah, I—'

Noah walked off without giving Scarlett a chance to speak. Damn. She'd have to apologise later. Her happiness at being the centre of attention dimmed at the thought she'd upset Noah with her careless remark.

'I think it's about time we made tracks,' said Sadie, 'Thanks for a lovely party, Scarlett and enjoy the rest of your day. It was great to see you again.'

Scarlett was grateful for Sadie's intervention. She had always been the sensible one; always the designated driver helping the others when they'd had too much to drink.

'We'll have to meet up for a catch-up. I was just saying that to Megs.'

'I'd like that very much.' Sadie beamed.

They hugged. Scarlett missed her friends. She didn't know where Sadie was working, whether or not she had a boyfriend. She hadn't been a very good friend and vowed to do better in future.

'I should get Megs home. Sadie smiled. Good old faithful Sadie making sure her friends were okay, thinking about herself last, if at all.

Sadie was the least selfish person Scarlett knew. She wished she was like her. This thought made her a bit tearful. That of course could be down to all the booze she'd drunk. But damnit, it was her birthday. Thirty-one years on planet Earth and what had she got to show for it?

'Scarlett, we're going now, too,' said Esme who looked stone cold sober. But she also looked happy; happier than she had done for years. Joel's arm was around her waist. He really loved her, and he wasn't afraid to show it. That was real love, wanting to be with the object of your affections no matter what.

She must have been staring. Lost in an alcohol-fuelled daze.

'Scarlett, are you okay?' Joel's gentle voice finally got through to her.

'Yes fine, just drunk. Sorry.'

'As long as you're okay,' said Esme.

'Of course. I was thinking how happy you look, Esme, and how thankful I am that you and Joel found each other. I can't wait for your wedding day, it's going to be so good.'

'Oh come here my darling sister.' Esme pulled Scarlett into her arms for a hug. She looked at Joel over Esme's shoulder and he was smiling, his gentle blue eyes twinkling.

Esme and Joel left and Scarlett wandered into the garden looking for Noah. He was throwing a frisbee for Crazy Boy.

'Having fun?' asked Scarlett.

'Yes, we are,' Noah said and threw the frisbee as hard as he could. The dog chased after it, a blur of black and white.

'I love dogs, they live in the moment. I wish we could do that instead of fretting about the future and regretting the past.' Scarlett's eyes filled with tears. Then she remembered the reason she was looking for Noah. 'I'm sorry about earlier, I didn't mean what I said.'

'So you don't think fancying me would be preposterous?' Noah's tone was light, but his jaw was clenched and his movements when he threw the frisbee were quick and angry.

Oh no, she'd really insulted him, hadn't she? 'No of course not. I just meant that we work together and... well, we're work colleagues. And friends. We are friends aren't we?' Was it possible Noah might want her to fancy him? No, why would he? He was an attractive man and would have no difficulty meeting women. She was just a work colleague and now connected by marriage. He had never shown the slightest interest in her before. Not in that way. She hoped this incident wouldn't affect their working relationship.

'Yes, Scarlett we're friends. It's okay, I haven't really taken umbrage. I was just joking.' That wasn't the impression Scarlett had got and she felt awful about it. He didn't look as if he was joking. He hadn't looked at her once and his jaw was clenched tight. He threw the frisbee so hard, it reached the bottom of the garden and Crazy Boy nearly crashed into the fence.

She hated upsetting people, especially those she liked. She invited him to the party so he could get to know everyone better and feel as if he belonged. And what had she done? Insult him. Not what she had intended at all. Especially as she did think he was an attractive man. In a dark, brooding kind of way. She could easily see why a woman would fancy Noah. Not preposterous at all.

'Good. So, no hard feelings?' She smiled at him, but his expression carried no hint of what he was feeling.

'None at all. Good to know we're on the same page.' Ouch. That was a bit of a kicker. But what did she expect? He had never given her any reason to think he fancied her. So that was good then, wasn't it. All cleared up. They both felt the same way about each other. Work colleagues. Nothing more.

The dog settled down with the frisbee between his paws, panting and waiting. He kept them in his sight the whole time, watching them with his beautiful dark brown eyes.

CHAPTER THREE

'Scarlett? Did you hear who was admitted last night?'

Scarlett had but wasn't in the mood for gossiping with the younger staff. 'I did, but the fact that she is a celebrity is irrelevant. We'll treat her the way we treat all our patients.'

'Of course. But it is exciting even so.'

Scarlett didn't think it was exciting. Well, maybe a little bit. After all, the celebrities usually went to the private clinics.

She still felt out of sorts after the misunderstanding with Noah at the party. She hated to think anything would affect their good working relationship. But now, she needed to concentrate on the new admission.

The patient had been treated for an overdose in the accident and emergency department and transferred to the secure unit of the psychiatric wing of the hospital. This patient had to be watched around the clock and monitored closely as there was a risk of her trying to take her life again.

Scarlett read her notes which consisted of a brief account of how she ended up in hospital. According to what was documented, her drinking had started the downward spiral.

Celine—not her real name—had been a famous soap star who had fallen on hard times when she began drinking heavily after a miscarriage. Once happily married she was now separated from her husband. Next to go was her job as she had turned up on set too many times falling-down drunk.

Then, the worse betrayal of all as she saw it, the gutter press turned against her. She had been a media darling—including social media—with followers on Instagram reaching the million mark, articles in glossy magazines, appearances on popular quiz shows and reality TV programmes. After the press printed photos of her falling out of nightclubs drunk and sitting on the kerb throwing up in the gutter, she soon became a laughing stock.

That was the start of a slow decline into obscurity. The press, when they bothered printing anything about her at all, claimed she had "lost it" and was a "washed out has been."

"Celine compares herself to Marilyn Monroe," the medical report read, "she knows she will end up dead as Marilyn did. High suicide risk."

Poor Celine thought Scarlett. She would need watching for some time. But that was what they were there for, to convince suicidal patients that life was worth living.

Scarlett pushed open the door to Celine's room and tiptoed in. There was a shape on the bed, covered in a duvet and blankets. An IV drip line snaked from the bag on the stand down to the bed and disappeared under the covers. Scarlett checked the line which was running normal saline before sitting down in a chair next to the bed.

The strong smell of vomit in the stuffy room and the closed blinds added to the feeling of claustrophobia. Scarlett wished she could throw open the windows and blinds and let in light and fresh air, but that would be the opposite of what Celine wanted at that moment. And the patient was the only one who mattered.

'Celine? Hi, I'm Scarlett, I'm one of the nurses. Do you feel like talking?'

As there was no response from the figure on the bed, Scarlett decided to give her another five minutes, so sat quietly saying nothing.

Just as Scarlett had decided to leave and try again later, the duvet was pushed away, and a head emerged from the bundle of bedding.

Scarlett got a shock when she saw Celine. She tried to hide her reaction so as not to upset the patient. Her face was lined, and she was completely bald. Her age was late thirties, but Scarlett thought she could have passed for sixty. Her skin was sallow and her eyes bloodshot. She was obviously dehydrated as her lips were cracked and bleeding. The poor woman was in a world of pain and Scarlett's heart went out to her.

'Who are you?' Celine's voice was hoarse as if she had a sore throat. That could have been from the tube they'd inserted in A&E.

'My name's Scarlett and I'm here to help you. Is there anything I can get you?'

'You can get me out of here, that's what you can get me.'

'We're here to help, Celine. You've had a bad time but you're in the right place now.'

'You want to help? I need a drink. Whisky.'

'Would you like some water?' Scarlett kept her voice calm but friendly. This was normal for some patients when they were first admitted. They tried to push the staff but, like young children, what they really needed was someone to take control.

'With the whisky? No, I drink it straight.'

'If you're thirsty, water is the best thing.' This was a battle she wouldn't let Celine win.

'If you're not willing to help me, what good are you?' Celine sounded angry but Scarlett knew it wasn't directed at her.

'We're all trying to help you, Celine, but you need to co-operate with us. Would you like to talk?'

'Not to you. I'll talk to the organ grinder, not the monkey.'

'I'm afraid the organ grinder is with another patient at the moment, but I'll tell him you're ready to talk, shall I?'

Celine lifted her head and stared at her. 'What did you say your name was?'

'Scarlett.'

'Scarlett O'Hara.'

'No, Scarlett McBride.'

Celine lay back down and pulled the duvet over her head. She spoke but her voice was too muffled to hear the words. Their conversation was obviously over and there were other patients to attend to, but at least she had made the first contact with her, and she had introduced herself. Slowly Celine would get used to her and, hopefully, learn to trust her enough to talk. It would take time, lots of time, but Celine wasn't alone and there would always be someone around to help her and listen to her when she was ready to confide in the staff.

Noah had read the medical report on new patient, Celine, but he was curious to know what her life had been like when she was at the top of her game, happily married and a media darling. He Googled her name and the site brought up hundreds of hits. He read that her husband, a musician in a mediocre band, had been indulging in affairs, taking drugs and disappearing for days at a time. He was ten years younger than Celine and unable to cope with her success.

Their marriage broke up after they'd suffered a miscarriage. It appeared that only Celine had suffered, he had got on with the business of partying according to social media, while Celine had turned to drink. A typical but tragic story.

Noah gazed out of the window, but he didn't see the grey sky, the cranes against the skyline as another bit of land in the hospital grounds was built on to house another department they desperately needed. The growing population and the advances in medical treatment meant that the hospital was in a constant state of expansion, attempting to keep up with the times.

But Noah didn't think about that, his thoughts had flown back to his early twenties when he had been a mere medical student desperately trying to balance his studies with long hours on the wards, lack of sleep and a social life that he didn't have time or energy to enjoy.

He too had turned to drink to get him through those early days he had found so hard to endure. Long desperate days when only the thought of the oblivion drinking offered stopped him from walking out of the hospital never to return. He had felt overwhelmed at the beginning of his training and had no faith in himself. Wanting to quit many times, it was only the thought of his father's disappointment in him if he had that kept him going.

He sighed as he remembered waking up after only a couple of hours sleep, dreading the following twelve hours on the wards, wanting desperately to drown his feelings of inadequacy in alcohol. He felt tired just thinking about it. He could still remember how pernicious that craving was and knew how easy it would be to give in to it. In those early days he had been permanently exhausted, existing on adrenaline and fear. Fear that he'd screw up and make a mistake. He had patients' lives in his hands and a wrong diagnosis, incorrect drug dosage or simple, plain incompetence could mean...

Noah mentally shook himself before he went further down the rabbit hole of his memories to deeper, darker events. By some miracle he hadn't killed any of the patients. It wasn't about him any longer. He'd survived and become a qualified psychiatrist so he could help patients like Celine. She was the important one now, he had to do his best for her. Letting her down would be unthinkable.

But he wasn't completely out of the woods. An alcoholic never was. How easy would it be to let himself be lured back to having just one drink? And one drink would lead to another, and then he'd be plunged back into the darkness, the hellhole of dependency. He mustn't let that happen. He needed to be on his guard at all times. Especially being near to where alcohol was sold, which was any social occasion. He'd managed his dependency by becoming something of a recluse. Avoiding clubs and pubs. But he was facing a challenging year with the stag night and the wedding. He needed to be extra vigilant. He'd come this far and wasn't going to give up now.

CHAPTER FOUR

Noah knocked on Celine's door, not expecting a response, but heard her call "come in", so he cautiously opened the door. To his surprise she was dressed and sitting in an armchair as if she had been waiting for him.

The curtains were open, and the room smelled of perfume.

'Celine, I'm Dr Noah Whittaker, how are you feeling?'

'I'm feeling fine. May I call you Noah?'

Noah disapproved of patients using the doctors' first names, but it was more important at this stage to gain Celine's trust.

'Of course. How have you settled in?'

'Oh, wonderfully well. I feel so much better, I'm sure I'm ready to go home now. Thank you for everything you and your team have done.' Celine's voice was rough as if her throat was raw. She tried to smile but it was a poor thing that didn't fool Noah at all.

Noah reminded himself that Celine was an actress. Her appearance belied her words. Her face was haggard and the make-up she had used to try to hide that fact just made her look clownish. Her eyes were red and swollen with dark circles underneath. She was a long way from being better.

Scarlett had typed a report of her first meeting with Celine that morning and added it to her electronic notes. No patient could have made such a miraculous recovery in such a short time.

'Do you feel well enough to talk?'

'Of course, what would you like to talk about?'

'I'd like you to tell me about yourself and the events that led to you attempting to end your life.'

'Oh, that was a mistake, I was feeling a bit low and took too many sleeping pills. I wasn't concentrating, that's all. No biggy.' Celine waved her hand and turned her head away.

'So you weren't trying to end your life?' asked Noah. He knew how seriously the staff in A&E had taken her "mistake". After they'd done a stomach washout, they'd referred her straight to the psychiatric unit.

'No, of course not, what gave you that idea?' She looked at him again but couldn't hold his gaze for long.

Noah realised that Celine was in denial, either because she really couldn't remember the events leading up to her hospitalisation, or she was playing it down so people believed she was well enough to be discharged.

He sat quietly for a few seconds, waiting for her to speak again, but Celine sat back in her chair with a serene smile on her face. A look designed to make him think she hadn't a care in the world? If it was, it wasn't working. Noah could see through it to the reality of her condition. Her hands shook slightly from alcohol withdrawal. Her skin was dry from dehydration. She wore a rather garish red wig which fitted badly as a result of the alopecia she suffered from. A condition that could be brought on by stress. Celine had suffered from more than her share of stress if all the stories about her were to be believed.

'So, when can I go home?' she asked trying and failing to smile. Her lower lip trembled.

Noah recognised the hint of desperation in Celine's voice and understood the importance of treating her gently. Despite not wanting to upset her further he needed to get her talking. The first priority for Celine was to encourage her to face up to the reality of her situation. Only then would she begin the long climb out of the dark well she'd fallen into.

'Tell me about your relationship with Troy.'

'Didn't you hear me? I asked when I could go home.'

Celine's voice had risen in her anxiety. She was obviously frightened of being in hospital and not being allowed to leave.

'You'll have to be here for a while, Celine. We can't let you go home until we're convinced you won't try it again.'

'Try what? I told you it was an accident.'

Celine's voice broke and she sobbed, a heart-breaking, helpless sound as if she had no hope left and was on the verge of giving up. The pain-filled sound made Noah instinctively want to comfort her, hug her, tell her everything would be okay. But he was her psychiatrist and had to keep a professional distance. Noah wouldn't let her give up. He wasn't prepared to lose a patient because he hadn't done enough to help her.

After a while Celine calmed down and she stopped crying. She stared at the floor and looked utterly defeated.

'Celine, I'll prescribe you some medication and I want you to take it, okay? I think it will help. I'll come and see you tomorrow and we'll talk.'

Celine nodded but didn't look up. It was going to be a long road to her recovery, but Noah was determined to help her get there.

When Scarlett entered the staff offices the following Monday, a young woman was standing with the ward manager, beaming. She was about five feet five inches tall, slim figure, long blonde hair with extensions that she wore in waves down her back and deep blue eyes. Scarlett stared at her, wondering who this stunning woman was.

'Hi, I'm Miranda, pleased to meet you.'

Scarlett shook her hand and studied her face. She had a perfect mouth with teeth that had obviously been professionally whitened, an oval shaped face, small nose, and small, neat ears with studs that could have been diamonds. Scarlett always noticed a person's ears. She didn't like her own very much—hers were too big— and envied women with neat little ears.

'Miranda is starting work today on the team and I wonder if you'd be good enough to show her around and meet the patients,' said the ward manager.

'Of course.'

'Oh thank you, that's so kind of you,' said Miranda.

'Where were you working before?' asked Scarlett. She'd love to know more about this new member of staff. Maybe she should offer to have lunch with her?

'I was in London, but I've worked all over the place.' Miranda laughed, showing her perfectly whitened teeth.

Scarlett introduced her to a single mother with bipolar who had a drink problem, a young man who had tried to take his life six times, an older autistic man who should be in sheltered accommodation but was waiting for a place, and others, mainly with alcohol or drug dependency.

'Right.' They stopped outside Celine's door. 'This patient is our celebrity superstar and is only with us until a place becomes available in a private clinic.'

'Oh, how exciting,' said Miranda, 'Do you get many celebrities?'

'Not often to be honest. They usually go to private clinics.'

'Of course.'

They went in to find Celine in bed with the duvet pulled over her head. This was obviously one of her bad days.

'Hi,' Miranda called in an upbeat tone of voice. Scarlett approached the bed and waited to see if Celine would respond. Miranda followed and pulled the duvet down so she could see her face.

'Hi, I'm Miranda, and this is my first day on the ward. I'm pleased to meet you.' She spoke too loudly as if the patient was hard of hearing. That wouldn't go down well.

Celine responded by lifting her head and looking Miranda up and down, then pulling the duvet over her head again. She was obviously having a non-verbal day which was Celine's sign to the world that she wanted to be left alone.

Miranda wasn't giving up and she sat in the chair that was strategically placed at the side of the bed and leaned forward.

'How about you come out from behind the duvet, and we can have a proper talk?'

Celine's response was to turn around in the bed, so her back was to Miranda. Scarlett knew it was hopeless to try to talk to her when she was like this and gestured to Miranda that they should leave.

'Maybe I'll sit here for a while. I'm sure I can get her to talk if we give her time.'

'I think it would be better if we came back later. I want you to meet the Consultant in Charge, Dr Whittaker.'

'Dr Whittaker. What's he like?' Miranda looked eager for information. She'd just have to find out for herself.

'He's very nice.' Three insignificant words that said nothing about the complex character that Dr Noah Whittaker was. Or at least that was how he came across to Scarlett. She was determined to get to know him better and discover the real Noah.

Scarlett knocked on his door and he called 'come in'. Noah looked up from his computer with a frown which changed to a smile when he saw who it was. Then when he caught sight of Miranda, he stood up, and walked around his desk towards them with his hand out.

'Hello, Miranda isn't it? Pleased to meet you. So glad you're here.'

'Hi, Dr Whittaker, I've heard a lot about you. It's so nice to finally meet you.' Miranda beamed her sunshine smile and Scarlett couldn't help noticing they held hands for longer than was normal. When had she heard a lot about him? She had just asked Scarlett what Noah was like.

'Call me Noah.' His voice was steady and his smile was open and friendly.

'Thanks. Okay… Noah.'

'All good I hope, the things you've heard,' Noah said with a nervous laugh. Scarlett had never known him to be nervous. Miranda was obviously having an effect on him.

'Oh sure,' Miranda said still smiling broadly. 'Everything I've heard about you is so positive.' Scarlett couldn't believe it, but Noah was blushing. She'd never seen that before either.

'Well, I'm flattered. I hope you'll be very happy here. Don't hesitate to ask if there's anything I can help you with.'

'Oh, I shall.' Miranda's voice had become husky and she stared up into Noah's eyes.

Scarlett stood apart watching the two of them, waiting for them both to remember she was there. Eventually they did, Noah with an embarrassed cough and Miranda looking as if she'd just met her prince charming.

Finally, Scarlett persuaded her to leave Noah's office and they made their way back to the ward.

'He's so good looking,' said Miranda, 'I wasn't expecting that.'

'You know when you said you'd heard a lot about him? Who were you speaking to?'

'When I came for my interview, they told me who he was and the wonderful work he does with mental health patients. And I googled him too, but his photo didn't do him justice.' Miranda giggled. 'He's so cute, I think I'm going to like working here.'

CHAPTER FIVE

N oah arrived home on Tuesday to the welcome aroma of food cooking. He realised how hungry he was as he wandered into the kitchen.

'Hi, Esme, that smells good.'

'Noah, hi. Just a simple meat and potato pie.'

'With pickled red cabbage?'

'Of course.'

'Great.' One of his favourite meals.

None of Esme's meals were simple; she was a wonderful cook. He'd teasingly told Joel that he'd need to be careful of his weight now he was enjoying Esme's three meals a day. Esme wouldn't want the Michelin man for a groom and the camera never lies.

It wasn't true, of course, his younger brother was built like a racing snake, there wasn't an ounce of fat on him. Joel had taken his advice to heart and had promised to start going to the gym with him. It would be nice to have some company.

'Shall I lay the table?'

'Thanks, Noah, that would be helpful. Can you lay it for four? Scarlett's joining us.'

'Sure.' So the feisty Scarlett was on her way. That'll make the evening more interesting. He wondered if she'd bring up the arrival of Miranda, the new nurse. He'd got a shock when he met her. The woman was beautiful. He hadn't been expecting that.

The doorbell rang and a few minutes later, Scarlett appeared carrying a bottle of wine.

'Hi, everyone!' she called. She stopped in the doorway to the kitchen as Noah finished setting the table. He preferred to eat his meals in the kitchen rather than the dining-room, it was more homely somehow.

'Scarlett—hello.' He wasn't sure what to do next. The spacious kitchen suddenly felt cramped with three of them in it.

'Noah. I bought some wine.' She handed the bottle to him, but Esme took it off him quickly.

'Lovely. Thanks Scarlett.' Esme smiled sweetly.

Joel arrived and said hello, then Esme served the meal. Noah sat down and concentrated on eating.

'This is gorgeous, hon,' said Joel.

'Yes, it is. I'll miss your cooking when I eventually get a place of my own and go back to living on take-aways.'

Noah had sold the house he'd bought and renovated to Joel and Esme and was living there as a lodger. He had promised them he would move out before the wedding but hadn't got around to finding anywhere. There was always the accommodation for medical staff at the hospital as a last resort. He hadn't lived on his own for a long time though and wasn't looking forward to it. He'd grown used to company and wondered if he would be lonely. He'd have to keep busy.

'You should learn to cook, it's not difficult,' said Esme sipping from her glass of water.

'I can cook, I just don't really enjoy it.' Noah drank from his glass of lemonade. Joel was drinking beer, also from a glass. Esme didn't like him drinking from a bottle or can. She was the kind of woman who inspired good behaviour. He grinned as he thought of Joel being kept in line by his fiancée.

'A new nurse started today. Her name's Miranda,' said Scarlett who had been quiet up to that moment.

'Good. The mental health sector is always short-staffed. What's she like?' asked Joel. He got up and took two cans out of the fridge, one beer and the other lemonade which he put in front of Noah, who popped the tab and carefully poured the lemonade into the glass.

'What did you think of her, Noah?' asked Scarlett. She was staring at him and her green eyes were like lasers.

Was that a trick question? He'd somehow had the feeling that he better be careful what he said. 'She seems very pleasant.'

'What does she look like? Is she attractive?' asked Esme. Could Esme read minds? Unless Scarlett had already told her about Miranda.

'I didn't really notice,' he lied.

'You did! She obviously made an impression. You were looking at each other as if all your Christmases had come at once.' Trust Scarlett to tell it like it is. She didn't sound happy about the situation. She was right, of course, Miranda had made an impression on him. A superficial one, of course, but he couldn't deny that he'd temporarily lost his composure.

'You, Scarlett, have a lively imagination.' Noah scraped up the last of his pie. 'That was delicious, Esme, thanks.'

'Coffee?' Esme asked.

'Yes, please,' said Noah.

'So… this nurse,' said Joel.

'Miranda,' Noah answered. How could he get them to change the subject? He didn't want Scarlett to know that he found her attractive.

'How attractive is she? On a scale of one to ten,' asked Joel. His baby brother was enjoying watching him squirm.

'We're not teenagers anymore, Joel. She's blonde and quite pretty.' That was honest enough.

'I thought you hadn't noticed,' Joel said grinning.

'I noticed that much.'

'I think you noticed a lot more,' said Scarlett. 'She's stunning, drop-dead gorgeous. Any man would have been bowled over by her.' Scarlett's voice had a catch in it and Noah couldn't help wondering if she was a tiny bit jealous of Miranda.

'I wasn't bowled over.' *Well, maybe a bit.*

'There's no shame in admitting you found her attractive as you clearly did. Just admit it.' Scarlett wasn't going to let this go. It was time to shut the conversation down as it was getting out of hand.

'Why? Does it matter? The only important thing is how she does the job and only time will tell us that.'

Esme made them coffee while Noah and Joel stacked the dishwasher. Scarlett sat at the kitchen table and tried not to think about Miranda. It had been obvious that Noah was impressed by her. She was sex on legs, any man would have been. So why couldn't he just admit it? And why did it matter so much anyway? It was nothing to do with her.

It had unsettled her seeing them together. Miranda said he was cute. He wasn't cute. Kittens were cute. Babies were. Dr Noah Whittaker was attractive, sexy, but definitely not cute. She needed to stop thinking about it. If she wasn't careful Noah would think she was jealous. And she wasn't. Not one bit.

When the coffee was ready they all made themselves comfortable in the living-room.

'Have you two got the stag night sorted?' Scarlett asked, as she sat in an armchair, her legs curled under her, clutching a cushion. She watched Noah as he relaxed in the other armchair. His hair stuck up at the front as if he'd been running his hand through it.

'Joel? Are we sure we only want a pub crawl locally?' Noah asked.

'Yes. Nothing fancy, just a quiet drink in the town centre,' Joel said.

'The answer to your question, Scarlett, is—yes, we have.' He looked over at her and grinned.

'And we want the same,' Esme said as she cuddled up to Joel on the couch.

'I can't help thinking we should spice it up a bit. I mean… a few drinks in the pub sounds awfully boring.'

'What do you have in mind?' asked Noah, 'Shall we all dress up as leprechauns and do an Irish jig?' His eyes were shining as he watched her as he sipped his coffee.

'Are you making fun of my party?' Scarlett felt mildly affronted at Noah's teasing. He should feel grateful he'd been invited never mind making sarky comments. Perhaps he was paying her back for the preposterous remark. Or her accusations concerning Miranda.

'I'm only joking, Scarlett, I thoroughly enjoyed your party and thought you looked adorable in your costume.' He grinned and his eyes were sparkling with mirth.

'Actually, a themed night would be a good idea. It'd bring a bit of sparkle and pizzazz to the proceedings. We could be characters from a film like Star Wars, or a group like the Spice Girls.' The three of them were staring at her blankly. 'Or, to continue the Irish theme, how about we go to the folk centre for a ceilidh night. Everyone loves dancing.'

'Scarlett, lovely as these ideas are, I can't see them going down well with the people I'm inviting.' Esme smiled at her affectionately.

'Well, maybe you're inviting the wrong people,' Scarlett muttered under her breath.

'How about it, Joel?' said Noah, 'Are you up for a ceilidh?' He leaned back in the chair and sipped his coffee.

'Sorry, Scarlett, we're going to be boring old farts and go to a couple of pubs for a quiet drink.' Joel smiled.

'Oh come on, Joel, you only get married once. You want to make the most of the chance to let your hair down. Live a little, be crazy.'

'Scarlett? I wonder if you'd do me a favour whilst we're away?' Esme asked.

'No problem,' Scarlett. She couldn't think what it could be, but anything Esme wanted from her she would gladly do.

'Would you help Noah look after the garden and house plants? Not that I don't trust you, Noah, but I know that gardening isn't something you've done much of. Just water and feed them and if you have time to mow the lawn that'd be great, but don't worry if you don't.'

'We'd rather like a wildflower meadow, wouldn't we?' asked Joel.

'Yes, we could think about that when we get back from our honeymoon,' said Esme.

Joel grinned. 'Yes, dear.'

Noah and Scarlett couldn't help smiling at them. They were so lovely together.

'Don't worry, we'll take care of everything, you go and enjoy your honeymoon. It's in our safe hands, isn't it, Noah?' She turned to him with a grin.

'As Scarlett says, you can leave it all with us.'

CHAPTER SIX

C andice and Frank McBride had chosen to get married in the spring; the second of April to be precise. Thirty-five years later, the McBride sisters had to find some way to help their widowed mother through what was obviously going to be a painful and emotional day for them all.

They decided to have a meal in Frank's honour. Scarlett looked around the room at her mum and sisters. They were all dressed up in pale blue, which was Manchester City's colours, the football team Frank supported all his life.

Candy had cooked roast beef and Yorkshire pudding, their father's favourite meal. Maria, who had just become a vegetarian, had the vegetables and potatoes.

The meal was a quiet affair, which was unusual for the McBride's. Usually when they all got together they competed to be heard. They all had things they couldn't wait to tell the others.

Today, there was a hushed almost reverential atmosphere. After the toast to Dad, they were silent, eating the meal slowly, occasionally glancing at the photograph of Mum and Dad on their wedding day that Candy had placed on the coffee table, surrounded by small vases of daffodils.

Scarlett stole a glance at her mother sitting at the head of the table. She smiled when she saw Scarlett watching her, so Scarlett smiled back.

Her mum looked okay, in control of her emotions but who knew how she was really feeling? Her eyes were bright, and she sipped her wine thoughtfully, occasionally glancing at the empty place at the other end of the table where her dad would have sat. The place was laid with a mat, cutlery, and an empty glass as if he was expected but was running a bit late and he'd come in soon, full of teasing, laughter, and love.

They each had a story to tell, a happy memory of their dad.

'It's your turn now,' said Connie, 'tell us what first attracted you to Dad.'

Candy gazed at the early evening light filtering through the curtains. 'He was a very handsome man and carried himself well. He always looked good in a suit. He looked a strong man and he was, physically and mentally, but he had the gentlest smile and the kindest eyes of any man I've ever met. As soon as I saw him I knew he was special, and I was right.'

Scarlett wondered if she'd ever feel like that about anyone. She was thirty-one and had never been in love. She'd thought she had been a couple of times, but when the relationship had ended she'd never given it another thought.

And now that Esme was marrying Joel, she would be next. At least that's what people said. "Your turn next" as if it was a foregone conclusion. No pressure then. She shook her head. She was supposed to be thinking about her dad, not herself.

The room fell silent as the five of them remembered Frank McBride in their own way. They stayed like that until the light faded and the day was over.

'Thirty-five years. It's a life sentence,' said Noah as he poured beer into one glass and lemonade into another.

'I know,' said Joel, stirring the pan of Bolognese sauce. Noah and Joel had decided to spend the evening together while Esme was with her family. 'A lifetime of being with the woman you love, having kids, grandkids and growing old together.' Joel drained the spaghetti, mixed it with the sauce and divided it onto two plates.

'Rather you than me, although I'm happy for you, it's just not something I want to do.' Noah watched Joel as he carefully carried the food to the table and they sat down.

Joel raised his glass. 'To marriage.'

'Or not,' said Noah, raising his glass. The sooner the wedding had come and gone, the better Noah would like it. Determined to play the part of best man for his brother, Noah knew how difficult he was going to find it.

They added parmesan cheese to the meal and got stuck in.

'How's the new nurse getting on?' asked Joel.

'Miranda? She's doing well.' Noah pushed the images of the nurse out of his mind. Gorgeous as she was, he didn't fancy her, not one bit.

'Have you asked her out?'

'No, and I don't intend to.'

'Why not? I thought she was beautiful and was charming all the men she met.'

Joel was grinning and Noah knew he wasn't going to let this go. 'She's a good nurse, and that's all I need to know about her.'

'Why?'

'She's not my type.' Noah didn't really have a type, but he was a red-blooded male and could appreciate a beautiful woman when he saw one. He just had no intention of doing anything about it.

'So… who is your type? Is it Scarlett, with that gorgeous red hair and green eyes?'

'No, it isn't. Anyway, she's not interested in me and before you ask, I know because I overheard her telling a friend that to fancy me would be preposterous. Her own words.' Noah's jaw clenched and he shoved the memory away. He didn't want to dwell on the thought that Scarlett didn't fancy him. He wasn't that bad was he?

'She said that? I'm surprised. I thought she liked you. In fact, I've always thought you'd make a lovely couple.'

'Well that just shows how wrong you can be sometimes. The trouble with being as loved-up as you are, is that you want to drag everyone else down with you.' Noah concentrated on eating his meal and didn't look up. He wished they could change the subject.

'I want everyone else to share in the joy of being in love. You know, spread the happiness around like confetti.'

'I'm happy for you, Joel, I really am, but not everyone wants to be in your situation.'

'So, when did you decide you didn't want to get married?' asked Joel taking a long drink of beer. He was lucky, he seemed to be able to drink several beers without any ill effects.

'It's not something I've ever thought about. I just don't see it as part of my future.'

'What do you see in your future? Being alone? Friends with benefits, serial relationships?'

Noah twirled spaghetti onto his fork and frowned. He stared at his plate as he answered. 'I'm not like you, Joel, I don't plan things to the nth degree. I don't intend to be celibate for the rest of my life, but I'm not looking for a wife either.'

'What if you fall in love?'

'I won't. I'm not the type.' He'd make sure he didn't by keeping away from beautiful women.

Joel drank his beer then was silent as he forked spaghetti into his mouth and chewed thoughtfully.

'Have you ever been in love?' he asked. His brother was obviously going to milk this conversation for all it was worth.

'To be honest, no. I've been in lust lots of times but never the total unconditional love that you feel for Esme and Candy and her husband must have felt for each other.'

'Wouldn't you like to be in love—you know, experience that eyes meeting across a crowded room scenario?' Joel smiled to show he wasn't making fun of him.

Noah sighed and pushed his empty plate away so he could lean his elbows on the table. He thought about how much to tell Joel. Perhaps he should tell him the whole story. Confession was supposed to be good for the soul.

'I don't think I'd be very good at it, I'm afraid. I'm too selfish. To have somebody who depended on me for so much of their well-being and happiness scares me, Joel. I know I'd let them down.'

Joel frowned and Noah wished he'd kept his mouth shut. He'd have to explain it all now, go back in time and relive the worse moment of his life.

'You've never let anyone down, Noah.' His brother had no idea. He sighed deeply and prepared himself to be strong. The image of a bottle of whisky floated into his mind and he pushed it away angrily.

'I have. Do you remember me going to a funeral when I was in medical school?'

'Vaguely,' said Joel, frowning.

'He was a close friend and fellow student. He'd been so happy and proud at the beginning. We all were. Wet behind the ears. None of us knew what was waiting for us. Once we were thrown in at the deep end, some of us survived and others... He told me he couldn't cope with the long hours, the study, the responsibility. He had decided to leave medical school because he couldn't stand it any longer. I told him not to leave because his father was so proud that his son was going to be a doctor.' Noah stopped not wanting to tell Joel how badly he'd stuffed up, but he had to be honest about what had happened. He picked up a knife, examined it and put it down again. *Just tell him.*

'Go on,' said Joel quietly.

'I was on nights and I'd been awake for about twenty hours as I had to work part of another doctor's shift. Dom and I shared digs with another student. I can't remember where he was.' Noah stopped, unable to go on as the image he had lived with for so long loomed over him and he couldn't shake it off. He ran his hands over his face, thinking that he needed a shave. How strange it was that in moments of high emotion and mental anguish, the mind still came up with trivia and the unimportant. Maybe it was the mind's way of protecting you from things that are too awful to face.

'Don't tell me anymore if it's too painful.' Joel's voice was quiet and calm. The voice of the physician to his patient. He shook his head and continued.

'Dom had taken an overdose and I found him. I couldn't revive him. I tried, I really tried…' His hands clenched into fists as he relived the feeling of desperation and terror he felt at finding his friend dead. He hadn't spoken about it for years and his throat closed with unshed tears. The ache in his heart overwhelmed him but he fought to continue. He didn't want to have to speak of it again.

'I gave him completely the wrong advice. You see, I struggled too when I was a student and the thing that stopped me from giving up was Dad and how ashamed he'd be of me if I quit. You know what he was like. We were a medical family and you and I were going to be doctors. But Dom wasn't me. I should have encouraged him to make his own decision, to do what was best for him. I should have supported him but instead I gave him the wrong advice and sent him over the edge.'

'You can't blame yourself.' Joel leaned forward and watched him closely.

'I can and I do. I know how Esme felt those ten years since her fiancé died. Guilt never really leaves you. I let Dom down in the worst possible way. I don't want to let someone else down like that. I couldn't go through it again.'

'But it wouldn't happen again because you've learned. You're a consultant psychiatrist, you understand about people's behaviour now, you were just a student then. Nobody could have expected you to know what to do.' Joel's argument was a good one and the temptation to believe everything he said and forgive himself was strong. But he'd lived with the guilt for a long time. It had been his fault. Dom died because of him.

'It doesn't alter the fact that my bad advice made a desperate man take his own life.'

'I think you're being too hard on yourself. And if you don't want to fall in love because you think you'll let the woman down then you really don't know what it feels like to be in love.' All the teasing had gone. Joel had his serious face on.

'You always hurt the one you love the most.' A cliché but true.

Noah got up, filled the kettle, and switched it on. Now that the memories had been raked up, he had a strong desire to give in and have a drink. One beer. But it wouldn't be just one, he wouldn't know when to stop. Tea would be better.

Noah made the tea and took another can of beer from the fridge for Joel.

'When I was with Julie I got hurt so many times because we weren't really in love. Now I'm with Esme, my true love, my soul-mate, my other half; all those expressions that used to be meaningless, I now know what they really mean. When I met Esme I knew that whatever life threw at us, we'd face together. That's the difference. When you're in love with someone who loves you back you'll always have someone to walk by your side.'

Noah looked at Joel's earnest expression as he tried to convince him that he was right. But he didn't want to think anymore of Dom or letting people down. There were too many painful memories to trip him up if they continued this conversation. He needed to get the talk back onto mundane things.

'Have you given any thought to arranging for our parents to meet Candy before the wedding?' If Joel was surprised by the abrupt change in topic, he didn't show it. He smiled and drank some of his beer.

'No, but that's a good point. They should meet. Esme's met them but that's as far as we've got.'

'Did that go well?' Noah relaxed now that they'd moved on to more pleasant things.

'Yes, surprisingly well. Esme's good with people, she always knows what to say. She won Dad over by admiring the garden and was gracious to Mum. Esme's got them eating out of the palm of her hand.' Joel's voice was full of admiration for his bride to be.

'So, now it's Candy's turn. How shall we play it? Their place or here?'

'I think we should check with Candy. It's two against one, don't forget.'

'Not if we include everyone. It'll make things easier on the wedding day if the two families have met.'

'A battle of the clans, God help us,' said Joel, 'I wonder which family will win.'

'My money's on the McBride's,' said Noah.

CHAPTER SEVEN

The Leytonsfield Hotel was not only the largest and oldest hotel in the town but was also the grandest and therefore a fitting venue for the two families to meet before the wedding. Candy had debated whether to have the meeting in her house and do another buffet. But she thought it would be nice to show the Whittaker's a bit of Cheshire history as the Leytonsfield Hotel was quite a popular landmark with the locals.

Scarlett made sure she was sitting next to Noah, so she could proceed with her plan to get to know him better socially and also so she wouldn't be bored out of her skull.

If it had just been the McBrides she would have had a great time. Her family knew how to have fun and no one stood on their dignity. Noah and Joel's parents—the senior Whittaker's as everyone was calling them—were a rum couple in Scarlett's opinion.

Desmond Whittaker was a short man but was quite the natty dresser. He wore a brown shirt and tie, with a tweed jacket and beige trousers. He had a handkerchief in the top pocket of his jacket. Unfortunately, his attire couldn't take away from his thinning hair and his watery blue eyes.

His wife, Kathleen, was tall and thin. She had wispy white hair and grey eyes, which made her look a bit colourless. Scarlett thought she could wear a deeper shade of lipstick which might help, but she wasn't about to suggest it to the woman.

As she tucked into her roast lamb lunch, Scarlett realised that Noah had hardly spoken.

'Are you alright?' she whispered to him.

'Yes. I'll be happy when it's over though,' he whispered back.

'Why?' asked Scarlett, sipping her orange juice. She and Noah had volunteered to be the designated drivers so was sensibly, in Esme's opinion, staying off the booze. Probably a good thing, she really didn't want to get drunk in front of Esme's in-laws.

'I hate this kind of thing,' whispered Noah. 'All the formality and stiffness. My father will want to be in charge of everything and my mother will find it all marvellous…'

'You sound bitter, Noah. Don't you get on with your folks?' She sat close to him, in order to talk without anyone else hearing. This nearness was both intriguing and alarming. Every time her gaze met his, her heart turned over in response.

'We get on well enough. My family aren't like yours.' Noah attacked his beef as if it was responsible for his mood.

'In what way?' Scarlett was even more intrigued now.

'Your family are natural. It's plain how much you all love each other and have each other's backs. With my family… well, we tend to stand on ceremony more. I don't mean we don't love each other, it's just that we hide it well.'

'How strange,' said Scarlett. Fancy wanting to hide the fact that you love your family. Scarlett could have shouted it from the rooftops, especially when something good happened. Esme meeting Joel, falling in love, and planning a wedding was the best thing that had happened to the McBride's for a long time. They were all genuinely delighted for her and didn't care who knew it. She'd been through so much and deserved to be happy.

'What do you think of Joel and Esme getting married?' She hoped he would be pleased for them. How could he be otherwise?

'I think it's great, really. They're perfect for each other and I wish them every happiness.'

Noah's words sounded rehearsed as if that was his stock answer when anyone asked him the question. What did he really think? Should she probe more deeply or leave it be?

Scarlett finished her meal and sat back in her chair.

'They'll be okay if you're worried about Joel. Esme adores him and he feels the same way. They're good together.'

'I agree.' Noah said. He drank some of his water and poured a glass for Scarlett. Instead of putting it in front of her, he handed her the glass and their hands touched, just for a second. It was unexpected and she felt as if she had been given a mild electric shock. Scarlett looked around the table to see if anyone had noticed and caught Joel's eye. He smiled and she returned it.

'So, tell me more about your business, Candy,' Desmond said.

So Candy told him about Candy Dots, the new coffee machine they'd invested in, plans for a café in the future, and he listened closely as if he was a potential buyer.

Kathleen was sitting on her own, twisting a paper napkin and looking around anxiously. Should she initiate a conversation? But couldn't think of anything to say so turned her attention back to Noah.

'What about this hen and stag night we'll be having? Strange we're having them on the same day.'

'Is it? You obviously know more about these things than I do.' He stared into the middle distance.

'All I know is that this night represents their last night of freedom and the purpose is to let your hair down and have fun. A couple of drinks in a local pub doesn't sound much fun to me.' She looked at him waiting for a response. He seemed to be thinking of what to say before he spoke. Scarlett took the opportunity to study his face. He frowned as if he had the weight of the world on his shoulders. What could she do to cheer him up?

'It's not about what we want is it? It's our job as best man and maid of honour to do the bidding of the bride and groom. And if they want a quiet drink, then we are obliged to provide that.' Noah spoke slowly and carefully as if he was speaking to someone of limited intelligence.

She kept staring at him, studying his profile. The set of his chin suggested a stubborn streak. He was an attractive man but would be more so if he smiled more often. He was still frowning.

'Do you know the origins of the hen and stag nights?' she asked sweetly. She was determined not to be upset by his patronising attitude. She was sure he wasn't really like that, he just felt uncomfortable for some reason. He turned his head then and looked her in the eye.

'I can't say I do. Do you?' he whispered.

'I'm glad you asked, Noah, because it just so happens that I do.' He grinned then and his eyes glinted with humour.

They were sitting so close together that their arms were touching. Maybe she should move away as she was obviously invading his personal space, but she didn't want to. She was perfectly happy where she was.

'Historically, hen was slang for women and stag for men.'

'Fascinating.' He was still watching her and his gaze dropped to her mouth.

'And there's more. The hen do dates back to Ancient Greek wedding traditions.'

'What about the stag do's?' He looked genuinely interested now and she felt warmth spread to her face by his direct stare.

'Mainly pub crawls. Men are not as imaginative as women.'

He laughed. 'I wouldn't argue with that.'

Scarlett was enjoying her conversation with Noah. He seemed to be a bit more relaxed now. Amusement danced in his eyes. She searched for something to ask him that would keep the conversation flowing.

'So... what would you do for your stag night?'

Instead of keeping the conversation flowing that question seemed to have killed it dead. Noah frowned and turned away from her. What had she said to annoy him?

'As I won't be getting married, that isn't something I'll ever have to worry about.'

'What? Not ever?' Why would he say something like that? Noah was a catch. A lot of women would be thrilled to win the heart of Dr Noah Whittaker. She needed to know what was behind this.

He sighed and drank some more mineral water. 'Not ever.' He spoke as if that was the end of the conversation. Move on or shut up. Scarlett had no intention of doing either.

'Why don't you want to get married, Noah?'

'I'd prefer to be free and single. I can't claim to be young anymore. I don't think I'd be very good at it, I'm afraid. I'm too selfish. To have somebody who depended on me for so much of their well-being and happiness scares me. I know I'd let them down.' Noah was frowning again and Scarlett wondered what was behind such a confession.

'But...'

Candy stood up. 'Can I have some hush, please? I just want to propose a toast. To Esme and Joel. Love and happiness my darlings. And a few grandchildren would be nice.'

They all laughed and everyone toasted Esme and Joel who looked pink cheeked and were grinning like a pair of fools. Scarlett wondered why Desmond hadn't proposed the toast, but then berated herself for that thought. It doesn't always have to be the man.

Noah was silent again. Her attempt to cheer him up and get to know him a spectacular fail. He looked more miserable than he had at the beginning of the meal.

CHAPTER EIGHT

Scarlett shepherded the hens into Mellow, Esme's favourite wine bar. She wasn't really a pub person and Scarlett knew she'd be happy here. Scarlett was pleased with the turn out for the hen night. When Mum had agreed to come too the numbers went up to fourteen. She was worried that somebody would be superstitious if there were thirteen hens.

'I love your dress, Scarlett,' said Nicole, Esme's best friend.

Scarlett, not wanting to be outdone by the younger contingent had bought herself the sexiest dress she could find. It was a green satin ruched mini dress and it clung to her like a second skin. And it had cost a bomb. As did the shoes.

'Thanks. Loving yours too!'

A hen night was a great excuse for the girls to wear their sexiest clothes. And if they didn't have anything suitable, an excuse to scour the boutiques in Leytonsfield town centre for the tightest, shortest and the most low-cut dresses they could find. The younger contingent had really gone to town with their sexy dresses, sparkly shoes with high heels, make-up that looked as if it had been applied with a shovel and bare legs that had been spray tanned a dark mahogany. There was glitter and bling everywhere Scarlett looked. Perfect.

'What d'you think?' asked Connie doing a twirl. She had spent hours in the hairdressers getting extensions fitted and was wearing a figure hugging red mini dress.

'You look amazing,' said Nicole.

Candy wore a dress with matching jacket in an oyster colour. Maria had played safe and worn her little black dress. Esme was in red and looked gorgeous as ever. Scarlett was disappointed that Esme hadn't liked the idea of a themed hen party as she could think of lots of characters she could have come as but was determined to stand out that night. Her sister, however, was much more sophisticated than Scarlett and looked elegant and graceful in her long, sleeveless dress.

'Okay ladies, come and get your sashes,' she called. She hoped she hadn't forgotten anyone. She handed out bride, mother of the bride, bridesmaid and hen party. She was already wearing the Maid of Honour sash. And hats with pink ribbon and badges that just said hen party. She could have spent a small fortune on more up-market merchandise, but her finances had taken a hit recently and she'd had to economise. She just hoped no one thought they were tacky.

Scarlett had feared that Esme wouldn't approve of how Connie and the other younger women, and herself come to that, were attired and order them all back home to get dressed properly, but she had underestimated how much her beloved Esme had changed since meeting Joel. The stern, prim and proper Esme of old had vanished to be replaced by a woman who glowed with an inner light, who smiled at everyone and who laughed easily and joyfully. It was as if Esme had been asleep for the last ten years and, like sleeping beauty, had been awakened by her sweetheart's kiss.

Perhaps fairy tales did come true. If that was what real love did for you, she approved. Not that she had ever felt it. Maybe she never would. That thought brought her up short like a gut punch. Was she destined to be alone for the rest of her life? *Get a grip woman.* She was determined to enjoy tonight and be part of making it a fabulous night for Esme.

'Right, what are we all drinking?' asked Scarlett who had collected money off them all except Esme to keep as a kitty to pay for drinks. They had all given generously, especially Candy who had given her a wad of notes to add to it.

'I want a porn star martini,' said Connie.

'Of course you do,' answered Scarlett dryly. With her Mum in attendance, she wouldn't have to worry about her baby sister getting drunk. Despite the fact that Connie was twenty-one and perfectly capable of making her own decisions, Candy would still look after her. And Scarlett would do too. She'd been looking after her and Maria all their lives and Esme had looked after all of them as far as she could. It came naturally to them all to look out for each other.

When they were all seated they drank a toast to Esme and Joel.

'Are you nervous yet, Esme?' asked Matilda, 'the big day's only a couple of weeks away.'

She grinned, but Esme just smiled. 'Not in the slightest. My wedding day can't come soon enough.'

There was more wedding talk from the older women; swapping wedding day disaster stories and talk about things to avoid and must haves but Scarlett zoned out. The party had split into two groups; Connie, Sally, Ebony, and two others she didn't know on one table and Mum, Esme, Maria, Nicole, Georgina, Aoife, Matilda, and Julie on the other.

Scarlett had been a bit surprised when Esme had added Julie's name to the list of hens. She was Joel's ex and at one time it seemed that she was trying to get him back. Esme had smiled and told her that she and Julie were friends now and she and Jon were an item.

'We need to think about moving on soon,' she said to Esme.

'Why don't we consider staying here for the rest of the evening? Now everyone has a seat and is settled.'

'Okay.' It made sense. The later the evening got the less likely they'd all get seats and everyone seemed happy where they were.

Scarlett couldn't help wondering where the stags were and what they were up to. She wasn't sure she was buying this no stripper, no funny business night they had insisted they were having. She wouldn't be surprised if they were at some strip club right now.

The stags had begun their pub crawl in The Station, which was situated on the edge of the town centre opposite Leytonsfield train station. It was a small pub and while not exactly a spit and sawdust establishment, was fairly basic and, apart from a dartboard, didn't offer much in the way of entertainment.

There were nine of them altogether; Jon, Richard, and Hamid from the medical centre, Patrick, Aoife's husband who had been delighted to be included, and Harry, Paul and Donald, friends of Joel's from Manchester.

They were all drinking beer except Hamid and Noah, who were on soft drinks, and Donald who was on whisky.

Noah wondered how the hens were doing. He was tempted to text Scarlett to see where they were, so they could avoid ending up in the same pub. But then... would it be such a bad thing if they did? Noah was craving a drink and needed a distraction. The familiar symptoms of restlessness, self-loathing and irritability were increasing. And would only get worse as the night went on.

The worst place Noah could be is surrounded by people drinking alcohol. Then, his brain tells him it's okay to drink and wants to be flooded with the good feelings that drinking gave him. He had to fight it. He wasn't going back to that place where he lived permanently at the bottom of a glass. He shouldn't be in a pub by rights. But he was doing this for Joel. He wasn't going to let him down. It was his stag night and Noah was determined to make it the best night he could. If his brother wanted a couple of drinks in the local pubs, that is what he would get.

'Right guys, drink up, we're off to the Grouse.'

The next pub was a slight improvement and they even managed to get a table, although they could only find five chairs so four of them had to stand. Noah stood as he felt too restless to sit. He checked his phone to see if there had been any texts from Scarlett but there hadn't been. Why he expected her to text him, he didn't know. Perhaps he just wanted her to.

After a short while, which felt like hours, he needed a drink again. The smell of the beer was making him feel queasy. It was ironic that the thing he craved wasn't something he enjoyed. He'd never liked drinking alcohol, the craving was for the feeling it gave him. The oblivion, freedom from thought and pain. *Oh for goodness sake, get over yourself.*

He looked around for Joel. He was standing talking to Patrick and it looked as if he was bending Joel's ear about something. Joel had warned him not to get Patrick talking about politics. He wandered over.

'Hey, you two, I've just had a thought. Why don't we move on to the Bull's Head, there's a beer garden and we'd probably all get seats, and it's a mild evening.'

Patrick frowned. He obviously didn't like being interrupted. Joel grinned.

'You're the boss tonight, whatever you say goes.'

'But you're the groom so you need to have a say.' Say yes, he willed his brother.

'Well, I say yes, great idea.'

'Good. Let's go then. Drink up guys.'

As they all knocked back their beer, Noah left his lemonade on the bar. It was sickly sweet and he would be better with mineral water for the rest of the night.

They meandered down Market street, chatting, laughing, and jostling each other. Perhaps he wasn't doing too bad a job after all. They all seemed to be enjoying themselves and no one had done anything embarrassing yet. Although the night was young.

'Let's have a selfie guys,' Joel said, 'with the pub in the background.' Normally, he would have done his best to escape being in a selfie. But this was Joel's stag night and if he wanted a photo of everyone to remember it by, then he would grin and bear it. Literally. Anything for his baby brother tonight and until he was married. After that he was on his own. The thought made Noah smile just as Joel took the picture. At least he'd be smiling on it, rather than scowling as he usually did on photos.

The hens looked as if they had dug in for the evening. No one seemed willing to move anytime soon. Mum, Esme, Nicole, and Matilda were deep in conversation about wedding dresses, Connie was chatting up the barman who seemed perfectly happy with the situation. Some of the younger women were drinking shots after failing to persuade Esme to join them.

Scarlett had just started to relax and accept that they would be here for the duration when the door opened and the last thing they needed came marauding into Mellow in the form of a group of men of various ages and states of inebriation. They wore scruffy jeans, even scruffier trainers, and white T-shirts with an obscene image of a man's genitalia which they probably thought was hilarious. Scarlett hoped their stags weren't as bad as this lot.

Scarlett glanced at Esme who was trying her best to ignore them. It was difficult, however, as they had annoyingly loud voices and half of them were singing lewd songs.

'Oh, for goodness sake,' said Matilda, 'I can't hear myself think.'

'That's just what we need,' said Candy, 'A group of drunken louts.'

'They're awful, aren't they?' said Scarlett. 'They're only going to get worse, I'm afraid, the more they drink.' Time to move on and as chief bridesmaid, it was her job to get them up and out. She wondered which pub the stags were in. Not that she was going to lead the hens there, she was just curious. She could always text Noah and ask him.

The drunkest of the men staggered over to their table and put his arm across Esme's shoulders. 'How about you and me have a bit of a practice run for your wedding night, darlin'. I can give you a few tips on how to keep your man happy.'

Because Esme was sitting down and he was standing leaning over her, she was trapped. Her serene composure had deserted her and she looked as if she was about to lamp him with the empty wine bottle.

'You're not the groom, are you?' asked Scarlett. God help the bride if he was.

'Me? Of course not. You wouldn't catch me getting married, darlin'. How about you? I've always loved red heads.'

'I think you should go back to your friends now, don't you? They'll be missing you.'

'How about we get together with yous? Are you up for a bit of fun, ladies?'

'Much as we'd love to accept your kind invitation, we have to leave now. But it's been a real pleasure meeting you. Come on, girls, let's go.'

'Nicely handled, darling,' said her mum.

Scarlett was delighted to see the hens draining their glasses and collecting bags and jackets. They couldn't get out fast enough.

CHAPTER NINE

M uch to Noah's delight, the hens arrived at the Bull's Head at the exact same moment that he was herding the stags into the pub.

'Well, hello you lot. What a wonderful coincidence.'

'Hello, Noah. What a surprise,' said Candy with a smile.

Now Scarlett was here, he had his distraction. He wouldn't be thinking about all the tempting alcoholic beverages he was surrounded by.

But when he saw her, he was speechless. He couldn't help staring at the vision of loveliness before him. He was gratified to see that she was wearing the silver locket and chain he'd given her for her birthday. Her hair was loose and flowed over her creamy shoulders. She wore a skin tight green dress that was so short it just covered her bum and so low that her cleavage was difficult to ignore.

Noah had never been one of those men who stared at a woman's breasts when he spoke to them but knew that tonight he'd have his work cut out keeping them up. He wanted a distraction didn't he? Well, now he'd got one. Be careful what you wish for.

Some of the men looked shocked to see the hens parade in, headed by the McBrides. Others looked pleased.

'Here she is, my little lady,' said Jon as Julie sashayed up to him.

'Hi lover,' she responded, 'Are you having a good time?'

'I will do now you're here,' he said as she threw her arms around him.

Joel and Esme were in a clinch and Patrick looked most put out as Aoife came up to where he stood with a huge grin on her face.

'You never said the wives were joining us,' he said with a frown.

'We've just escaped the clutches of a stag party in Mellow,' said Georgina, 'And now we've bumped into you lot.'

'I think we're quite safe with these stags,' said Scarlett, 'Wasn't sure about the other guys.'

'They were so uncouth,' said Matilda shuddering delicately.

'Did you plan this?' asked Patrick obviously still put out at having his all male evening ruined.

'Of course not,' said Aoife, 'We live in a small town, it was bound to happen.'

'Hi, Scarlett, nice to see you. Are you having a good time?' said Noah.

'Nice to see you too. And yes, I am.' Scarlett stared up at him, her eyes blazing green fire and a determined set to her jaw. Her lipstick was bright red which meant another part of her body he couldn't take his eyes off. Noah had never seen her looking as gorgeous as she did at that moment and he felt stirrings that he would rather not have. He needed to calm down.

'Right. Let's get the drinks in.' Noah rubbed his hands together and tried to remember what the men had been drinking.

Once everyone had found seats outside and had a drink in front of them, Noah looked around for somewhere to sit and found the only empty seat was next to Scarlett.

'So, how's it going? Are you all having fun?' asked Noah, determined to keep the conversation light and cheerful.

'I've had no complaints so far. How about you?'

'What? Complaints? No, none so far.'

'Well, at least that's one job that we can tick off the list,' said Scarlett.

Noah agreed, not wanting to admit that he was worried sick about the wedding and the best man's speech. He was no good at stuff like that and didn't want to mess it up.

'Why aren't you drinking Noah?' A question he dreaded. This wasn't the venue for confessions. He forced himself to smile and act nonchalantly.

'I like to keep a clear head when I'm out.' It was as good an excuse as any and someone had to stay sober.

'Very wise,' said Scarlett, nodding. He noticed that she wasn't staying sober. Her glass of Prosecco was half empty already.

It was a clear night with a half moon and a cloudless sky full of stars. They'd been lucky with the weather. You never knew with Spring, it could go either way.

'Even though we've worked together for a few years, I don't know much about your private life, Noah,' said Scarlett. She was looking at him quizzically as if she was trying to work him out. Good luck with that one.

'What do you want to know?' he asked, hoping he wouldn't be dragged into a serious conversation about his childhood or hopes for the future.

'I don't really know exactly. I think that, as we work together, we should know each other better, that's all. And the fact that you'll be my brother-in-law.'

'Okay. Why don't you tell me about you. Who's the real Scarlett McBride?'

'I am. I'm an open book with no secrets. I like good food, wine, fast cars, being with family.' Scarlett stopped and Noah sensed she wanted to say more but had stopped herself.

'Fast cars? What do you drive?' Noah felt he should know this, as they both used the hospital carpark, but surprisingly he didn't.

'An Audi. Do you know these places that advertise cheap but affordable fast cars? Well, they're lying. If it's fast, it's expensive.'

'So, what car would you buy if money was no object?'

'A Ford Mustang. Love them.' Scarlett's expression told Noah all he needed to know. Just the thought of her favourite car had produced the most beatific smile. 'What about you?'

'Me? Oh, let me think.' He also loved fast cars and knew the cars he loved the best were out of his league. But if he could buy whatever he wanted, it would be… 'Lamborghini. One of the Aventador models would do me.'

'Oh yes, good choice. Very nice,' said Scarlett approvingly.

'Well, that's something I've learned about you, Scarlett.' He would never have guessed that Scarlett was a speed freak.

'Your turn. Tell me something about you.'

What could he say? This wasn't the time or place to tell her he was a recovering alcoholic. His mind was blank and he was just starting to panic when Esme wandered over.

'I think we're going to call it a night. Thank you, you two for a lovely hen and stag night. Maria and Mum are coming with us, but I think the young ones are going on to the Late Club.'

'Okay. I'm glad you enjoyed it, Esme. Love you.' Oops. Scarlett realised she was slurring her words slightly. Maybe she should switch to soft drinks. She really didn't want to get drunk in front of Noah who was stone cold sober.

'Love you too. Goodnight.'

A young man had joined the group and was dancing with Connie. They both had earbuds in and the young man held his phone, obviously the source of the music.

'Who's the young guy?' asked Noah.

'His name's Matt. He's a bartender at Mellow and Connie seems to have picked him up.'

'I think I'll go and find out what everyone's plans are.'

'Do you want me to come with you?'

'No, it's okay, you stay here, I'll be back in a minute.'

Scarlett watched him walk away. Her boss was a handsome man and he obviously frequented the gym to have muscles like those. But he was full of secrets and she wished she knew why he didn't drink. Not because of religion, maybe health. Perhaps it was exactly as he'd said—he simply planned to keep a clear head.

Noah started walking back. Scarlett looked at her phone so he wouldn't think she'd been staring at him, even though she had.

'The young ones are going on to a club. Do you fancy it?'

'No, I think I'll go home too.' She didn't want the night to end but it had been ten years since she'd been a regular clubber and she didn't think Connie and the younger women would appreciate her chaperoning them like an old maid in a Jane Austen novel.

'I'll walk you home.'

'Okay. Thanks.' The fresh air might sober her up. She linked him and the two of them strolled in the moonlight through the deserted streets.

'I've enjoyed tonight,' said Scarlett.

'Me too. More than I thought I would. Glad it's over though.'

'You know, if you need any help with your best man's speech, you only have to ask. I can give you all the gen on Esme.' Not that Scarlett doubted his abilities to write a speech, but they should work together seeing as they were the best man and maid of honour.

'That's kind, Scarlett. I'll let you know if I'm struggling,' he answered softly.

Half way back, Scarlett's stilettos had rubbed her heels raw and she took off her shoes.

'What's up?' Noah asked.

'My shoes are rubbing so I've taken them off.' And if he said anything he'd regret it.

'You can't walk through the streets in bare feet. I'll carry you.'

'What?! Carry me—are you mad?' He had to be joking. She started laughing and couldn't stop. Maybe she hadn't sobered up after all.

'Don't you think I can do it?' Noah had a challenging note in his voice.

'No I don't. Not all the way.'

'I'll give you a piggy-back, so get on.' He turned around and bent down slightly.

'No one's said that to me in a long time.' She put her arms around his neck and he held her legs on either side of him. Her shoes dangled from her fingers. She hoped she didn't drop them, they'd cost her a fortune.

They used to do this as kids. But the feelings that surged through her were adult. All grown-up feelings. Feelings she probably shouldn't be having. She clung on tight and closed her eyes, inhaling the scents of the night and listening to Noah breathing. The feel of his hands on her bare legs played havoc with her erogenous zones. She had an overwhelming desire to giggle.

Noah moved with ease despite the weight he carried. Scarlett hardly ever weighed herself, but she knew she wasn't a light-weight. He didn't seem to be struggling at all. His hands on her legs were dry, so he wasn't sweating. His breathing seemed normal.

'You okay, Noah?'

'Fine thanks.' His voice was perfectly normal. Not out of breath. How impressive.

Too soon, as far as Scarlett was concerned, they reached her home. Maria was already in as there was a light on downstairs.

He stopped and she slid off him. 'Well done.'

'All those gym sessions must have paid off.' He stood in the light from the house and watched her.

'Well, thanks for walking me home. I mean carrying me home. I'd invite you in for a coffee but it's a bit late.'

Noah smiled. 'Another time maybe?'

'Yes, definitely. Noah?'

'Yes, Scarlett.'

'I don't think it would be propisterous... I mean preposterous for me to fancy you. I'm really sorry I ever said that. It was stupid and I hope you don't think—'

Noah put his finger gently on her lips. The warmth of his touch flooded her and she leaned in slightly. Would he kiss her? Did she want him to? Was she still drunk?

'Go in now Scarlett. Sweet dreams.' His voice was gentle and she didn't want him to leave.

'Yes. You too. Night.'

'Night.'

Noah waited until she was inside. She stayed in the hallway until she heard the gate click shut. He was gone.

CHAPTER TEN

'Hurry up, I need a wee,' shouted Connie, banging on the bathroom door.

Did she though? Or was that just a ruse to get her out of the bathroom? Scarlett had sneaked in as the rest of them were finishing their breakfast. Scarlett decided not to risk it and opened the door.

'Thank goodness,' Connie said as she pushed past her.

The wedding day had finally arrived. Esme had stayed with Scarlett and Maria the night before and Candy and Connie joined them the next morning. Now, they were all trying to get ready while sharing one bathroom.

Eventually Scarlett finished everyone's make-up and, amidst all the teasing and joking, they managed to get ready and gathered together in Esme's old room for a selfie.

They all fell silent as Esme twirled for them in her wedding gown.

'Oh, darling, you look absolutely gorgeous,' said Candy. Her voice was husky and her eyes were wet.

'Wowser,' said Connie.

Maria had tears rolling down her cheeks and Scarlett was speechless.

She had gone with Esme to choose her dress and the bridesmaid's dresses so knew how she had looked when she first put it on. But now, with her hair freshly washed and styled and her make-up on, she looked amazing.

The dress was a simple style and could have appeared rather plain on a woman who didn't have Esme's height, her beautiful long legs and slim figure a model would envy. The dress had a cowl draped neckline, and a leg slit so she could show off her bridal shoes.

The bridesmaids wore floor length chiffon dresses in a slate blue with spaghetti straps and an identical leg slit to Esme's.

Candy had chosen an evening gown with lace applique in the same shade of blue as the bridesmaid's dresses.

'Goodness, we're an attractive lot,' said Connie posing in front of the mirror. Joking aside, Scarlett had to agree with her. Everyone looked amazing, but it was Esme who stole the show. Esme was a beautiful woman and Scarlett could have wept with happiness for her. She'd found her Prince Charming in Joel and now her life could really begin.

Esme and Candy rode in the first car with the three sisters in the second. Connie kept getting the giggles as Scarlett waved out of the window like the Queen. It was amazing how many people stopped to stare at them. A lot of them waved back. People love a wedding.

The atmosphere changed when the cars stopped in front of the church. This was real. It was really happening. Organ music was entertaining the congregation until they arrived.

They began the procession into the church and the organist changed the music to the wedding march. Connie and Maria first, followed by Scarlett, then the bride and mother of the bride. So they were doing things a little differently, so what? It was Esme's wedding and whatever she decided was the way it was going to be.

When Scarlett approached the altar she cast her gaze over the Whittaker brothers looking smart in their wedding finery. Joel looked taller as if his feet weren't touching the ground. Noah looked composed, his expression solemn.

The congregation had turned to look at Esme, following on sedately with Candy. There were murmurs and "oohs" as they gazed at Esme holding her roses and outshining any model that ever lived, and the Mona Lisa come to that. There never was a more beautiful bride than Esme.

Scarlett kept her gaze on Joel as he saw his bride in her dress for the first time. She had expected to be amused by the adoration on his face, but the look of love he gave her, oblivious to everyone around him, brought tears dangerously close to the surface. She concentrated on taking Esme's flowers without dropping them and she was so relieved when she could sit down as she was starting to feel a bit faint. Perhaps she should have eaten breakfast, instead of just having a cup of tea.

After the "Dearly Beloved…" she stopped listening. She let her mind wander and it took her to a place she didn't really want to visit. Noah. Had he been about to kiss her when he had carried her home from the hen night? She'd been convinced he would and was ready. But he hadn't. The disappointment she felt had surprised her. She had to admit to herself that she thought he was very attractive with his dark brown eyes and dark hair. And the way he seemed to permanently have a five o'clock shadow… Did she just admire him? Or were her feelings involved? The jury was still out on that one.

Scarlett heard the vicar giving Joel permission to kiss Esme and there was a general wave of "Ah's" as he obeyed with relish. Then it was over, and they were grinning as if they'd just won the lottery as they made their way down the aisle to the doors where, no doubt, the whole wedding party would be showered with confetti.

At last the ceremony was over and they were all happily seated in the venue room of the Leytonsfield Hotel. Noah wished they could get the speeches over with first and then he'd be able to enjoy the wedding breakfast. His nerves were wound as tight as guitar strings and his stomach gurgled like a drain. Maybe he should have eaten breakfast after all. No matter how much he told himself he was being stupid his body wouldn't listen and portrayed all the symptoms of extreme stress.

And the worst thing of all—he desperately wanted a drink.

The wedding party were seated at the top table; Joel and Esme in the middle with Candy, Maria, and Connie on their left and on their right, Scarlett, himself, his mother and his father on the end.

With Scarlett sitting so close to him, his thoughts turned to the hen and stag night. He'd enjoyed proving to Scarlett that he was strong enough to carry her home. And he'd come close to kissing her when they had said goodnight. He'd wanted to but fortunately common sense had prevailed. She'd been drinking and he was trying to look out for her not seduce her. They were work colleagues and friends. That's all.

'Are you okay, Noah?' asked Scarlett.

'No. I feel sick. I should have taken you up on your offer to help with the speech. I still don't know what I'm going to say.' He sipped some water in an attempt to settle his stomach.

'What have you got so far?' Scarlett asked.

'Not a lot. I'm trying to be witty. The best man's speech is supposed to be funny.' It sounded pathetic as he said it. He was feeling pathetic at that moment and *really* wanted a drink.

'I think you're funny.'

'Do you?' Was she teasing him, or did she mean it?

'Well, you make me laugh.'

'Thanks for that vote of confidence.'

Despite the nerves, Noah still registered how beautiful Scarlett looked in her bridesmaid dress. He'd seen pictures of brides and their bridesmaids looking like meringue's on legs. The McBride women looked sophisticated, polished and beautifully chic.

'I think it's more important to be sincere than to be funny. Joel is your little brother, and you want the best for him. And you're delighted that he's found the best in Esme. You could touch on how much he means to you. Something along those lines.'

Noah couldn't tear his eyes away from Scarlett. 'You're a genius. I don't suppose you'd like to rewrite my speech for me would you?'

Scarlett grinned. 'You'll be fine. Just speak from the heart.'

The first course was served and Noah managed to eat it. The rest of the meal passed too quickly, and Candy stood up, tapping her spoon on the side of a glass to get people's attention. Her speech was short and to the point. She thanked everyone for coming, told them how delighted she was that Esme and Joel were together and proposed a toast to the happy couple.

And then it was his turn.

Noah cleared his throat, stood up and began. He thanked the guests for coming and sharing this special day with them. He thanked Candy and the bridesmaids and Maid of Honour.

'I was really nervous about giving this speech today until a wise woman told me to speak from the heart. So here goes.' Everyone was listening. He glanced down at Scarlett, and she smiled and nodded.

'Joel is very special to me. He's my baby brother. My only brother. My only sibling.' There were a few titters from the guests. He nearly said that the only sibling they knew about but after glimpsing the mutinous look on his father's face he decided against it. He wasn't happy at being seated on the end with only his wife to talk to.

'I want the best for him, and I'm happy to say that he has the best in Esme. Life hasn't been easy for these two people but through all the adversity and bad times, somehow they found each other and fell in love. I've never seen Joel as happy as he is today and it's all down to the lovely lady who is now his wife.'

Please raise your glasses and join me in wishing Joel and Esme long life together and abundant happiness. To Joel and Esme.'

'To Joel and Esme' resounded around the room and Noah collapsed onto the chair, amazed and grateful that he'd done it.

'You were great. Well done,' said Scarlett beaming at him.

'Thank you for telling me what to say.' He owed a lot to Scarlett for her help and support. He didn't think he would have got through it if she hadn't been sitting next to him.

'It was a pleasure. Would you like some champagne?'

'No, I'll stick to water.' He needed a drink, desperately, but wasn't about to undo all the good work he'd done that day by having one drink. He was incapable of only having one.

'Don't you drink at all, Noah?'

'Not any more. Not since my student days.' He had been thinking of telling Scarlett that he was a recovering alcoholic. As they treat so many people at the unit with the same problem it seemed wrong somehow to keep it from her. He wasn't ashamed of it—well, maybe a bit—if anything he was a walking billboard for the fact that it can be overcome. He hadn't planned to tell her at the wedding though.

'Is it... you know?'

His heart hammered against his ribcage. Despite what he'd just been thinking, he couldn't help feeling that telling her about his addiction was admitting how weak willed he was. 'Yes, I was an alcoholic.' There, he'd said it. His secret was out in the open and the world hadn't come to an end. He felt relieved. His palms were sweaty and he wiped them on his trousers.

'I'm sorry. Did you go to AA and all that?' Scarlett hadn't recoiled in horror. He felt happier talking about it with her.

'No, I had a student counsellor to talk to, but I went to a few later on when I was tempted to drink and didn't think I could resist. I'll tell you all about it one day if you like.'

'Yes, I would like to hear it.'

'I'd be grateful if you'd keep it to yourself though.' Scarlett was sympathetic but he wasn't sure about the rest of the people they associated with.

'Of course. I won't say a word.' She smiled at him and he couldn't help feeling that a weight had been lifted.

'What's next?' he asked, amazed that he'd done the speech and it seemed to have been well received. He could relax now and enjoy the rest of the day.

'The bouquet tossing,' said Scarlett pulling a face.

'Is that like tossing the caber? Only with flowers? Noah felt in a better mood now the speeches were over.

'It's when all the single women and men—let's not be sexist—fight amongst themselves to be the lucky one who catches the bride's bouquet. Whoever catches it will be the next one to be married. Saddo's.' Scarlett shook her head as if she couldn't believe people could be so stupid.

'Don't you want to get married some day?'

'I don't know. Someday, a long time in the future maybe. I've never been in love, so I can't imagine wanting to spend the rest of my life with just one person. But I'm not superstitious enough to think that catching a bunch of flowers will make any difference.'

So, she'd never been in love. He was surprised. Such a gorgeous woman must have had her share of men wanting to take her out. But none of them had won her heart.

Esme stood up and walked over to where the bouquet toss would take place. A small group of hopefuls had already gathered there.

Joel leant over and said, 'Scarlett? I think Esme wants you to join them.'

'She knows me better than that.'

Noah looked over to where a good crowd of eager women were waiting. Esme was gesticulating and pointing to Scarlett.

'She wants you to get off your bum and join in the fun,' said Noah. He couldn't stop a chuckle from escaping.

'I don't believe it,' said Scarlett as Candy, Maria and Connie got up and joined the other women.

'Well, that's it,' said Noah, 'You'll have to get up now, otherwise you'll be the only McBride still sitting down. Imagine the shame.'

'Oh damn,' said Scarlett and Noah felt her pain even though he found it hilarious.

'And the photographer's getting ready to snap an action shot.' Noah laughed as she got up and reluctantly joined her family.

CHAPTER ELEVEN

S carlett reached the group of women wondering how she could keep out of the way when Esme threw her flowers. The photographer was moving around trying to find the perfect spot and avoid the stilettoes and elbows of the almost frenzied women.

'You took your time,' said Connie, 'Esme was waiting for you.'

'Well, I don't know why she bothered. I'm not going to catch it.'

'Don't worry, I will,' said Connie with a grin.

'Hush girls and get ready,' said Candy who was obviously loving the drama of the occasion.

Esme looked over her shoulder and threw the bouquet high and wide to exactly where Scarlett was standing.

'Catch it, catch it!' shouted Candy in an extremely embarrassing fashion.

The photographer was busily snapping the action.

Scarlett had no choice as the bouquet landed squarely in her hands. She hadn't even had to move. Esme had aimed for her, and it was a perfect throw.

'Well done, darling. All those years when Esme was captain of the school netball team have paid off.'

Connie and Maria had gone back to the table, and Scarlett could see that Connie was in a huff. She hated losing, especially to Scarlett.

Now she had to join the wedding party where she'd be subjected to teasing and jokes from Noah. And she'd been enjoying herself up until this stupid bouquet toss. She was hearing Noah's secrets and felt grateful that he trusted her enough with the big one. She wondered what other secrets he was keeping.

'Congratulations,' said Noah as Scarlett threw the flowers on the table.

'What for? I never wanted them in the first place,' said Scarlett avoiding eye contact with Noah.

'They're cutting the cake now. Do you want to join them?'

'No thank you. I'll just sit here for a bit.' She picked the petals off the roses in her bouquet and lined them up on the table. They felt like soft velvet. The smell of roses wafted upwards and she breathed deeply.

People were gathering around a table where the six-tier wedding cake slaved over by mum and Dot stood. Guests admired it and took photos.

'What's wrong, Scarlett?' Noah asked gently. 'And don't tell me nothing as I know you too well to not recognise when you're upset.'

He thought he knew her well. How? They'd only just started socialising as a family. They'd worked together for six years and now were related by marriage, but Scarlett didn't feel she knew Noah well at all. She wanted to. But he thought he knew *her* well. Was he right?

She couldn't tell him the truth, that when she caught the bouquet, she had a sudden image of Noah smiling at her. Of all the men she could have conjured up in her mind's eye, why did it have to be Noah? She glanced at him watching her, a five o'clock shadow just starting to appear, his brown eyes deep and soulful and a smile playing around his mouth.

She had wanted him to kiss her and still did. There was no point denying it. She hadn't wanted Megs to make a play for him because… yes, she did want him for herself.

'Or, if you don't want to talk, we could always go and eat cake.'

Scarlett laughed. 'They won't let us eat it yet. We'll get a piece at the end of the evening in a small box to take home.'

'Okay, I'll wait. I'm a patient man.' What else would he wait patiently for?

'Have you ever been in love, Noah?' He was lounging back in his chair, his finger running up and down his glass of mineral water with a pensive look on his face. She wanted to know more about him. What made him tick? What did he really want from life?

'I thought I was once, but it didn't last.'

'Why don't you want to get married?'

'Hey, what is this? Twenty questions?' He laughed and gave her a searching look.

'Sorry, I thought with us talking in the middle of a wedding it seemed like a reasonable question to ask.'

He had the grace to smile. 'You're right. Okay, well, I don't want the responsibility of someone depending on me for their happiness and security. I'm not sure I wouldn't let them down.'

'Why would you let them down?' Noah was one of the most trustworthy people she knew. Maybe he was a commitment phobe as well as a recovering alcoholic. Perhaps the two were connected.

Noah didn't have time to reply as Esme and Joel got up for the first dance.

'Oh, it's a waltz. Esme's been teaching Joel. He's good, don't you think?'

'My baby brother's good at most of the things he does.'

Soon after the wedding party were called on to the dance floor to join the bride and groom. When they got there Noah pulled Scarlett into his arms. The sudden movement caused her heartrate to shoot up and she couldn't catch her breath.

They weren't doing any dance steps that Esme would have approved of, but as she was otherwise engaged, gazing into the eyes of her new husband, they could be breakdancing for all her big sister would care. As it was, Scarlett felt as if she was floating rather than dancing, gliding, her feet hardly touching the floor.

Noah was holding Scarlett tightly against him and she had her left arm firmly around his neck. Instead of avoiding eye contact to prevent embarrassment as she would have done if she'd been dancing with anyone else, they were gazing into each other's eyes as if they could read the other's thoughts.

Her insides quivered as his gaze travelled over her face. She felt wrapped in an invisible warmth and a delightful shiver ran through her. She'd never felt so turned on and wanted this feeling to go on forever. Her sensible mind told her to resist, but her reckless body ignored it. He was all male and she was under his spell.

He had taken his jacket off and his muscles rippled under his white shirt. He moved with easy grace and Scarlett wondered if he'd done a lot of dancing. His hand held hers gently but firmly as he guided her around the room. She had no idea what dance they were doing, but she never wanted it to stop.

Scarlett loved dancing and followed his movements easily. They were together as one and she wished the dance would go on all night. Her breathing quickened as she dropped her gaze to his mouth. Sensual lips drew her in. What would he do if she kissed him now? His gaze had never left her face and she wondered how the day would end. She knew how she wanted it to end; in Noah's arms.

Scarlett felt she was in a dream and any minute she'd wake up and be sitting at the top table alone with the wilting table decorations and the abandoned glasses of flat champagne that were losing their bubbles and their appeal.

But no, he was here gazing at her with a quizzical look, as if he wanted to say something but couldn't quite make up his mind whether to or not.

When the song ended everyone in the wedding party went to sit down, except Noah and Scarlett. She couldn't tear her gaze away from him. Her fingers ached to touch his face.

Eventually he moved away from her with a smile and gestured that he was going to the bar. She stood watching him, wondering what the heck had just happened. She'd never felt like that about any man before. An overwhelming need had spread through her body like fire, rending her incapable of speech or movement. She wandered in a daze back to the table.

Maria came over to talk to her.

'How are you enjoying the wedding?' Scarlett asked her trying to smile at her younger sister.

'It's okay, but I'm feeling tired now. I think me and Connie will go after we've waved Esme and Joel off.'

'Okay.'

'Would you mind being alone tonight? Mum's asked me if I want to go home with her and Connie. Unless you want to come too?'

'No, I don't mind and I'll be fine.'

'Are you sure? You'll be alone in an empty house.' How like Maria to worry about her like that. She was always thinking of others.

'It's all good, really. I'll be okay.' She wondered what plans Noah had. He would also be alone in an empty house as Esme and Joel would be leaving for the airport to start their honeymoon soon.

There was great excitement in the hotel lobby and shouts of "They're leaving!" Noah had returned and offered her a hand. She took it and let him lead her to the hotel entrance so they could wave goodbye to their siblings.

Joel and Esme had gone. His parents had gone, saying they had a long drive back to Stoke on Trent. The McBride's had gone home.

Noah had anticipated feeling a bit lost and lonely when everyone had left, and he would have done if it wasn't for the sparky redhead by his side.

It was the end of the evening, the time for them to leave. Despite the tension he'd felt all day, he was reluctant to go home. The main reason was the fact that he could easily give in to his craving and have just one drink which would lead to just one bottle and then he'd be lost. One of the reasons he hated being alone was that he didn't trust himself.

But the alternative was to invite Scarlett back for a coffee. Bad idea. She was gorgeous, sexy, a little bit drunk, but sobering up with the mineral water he'd been giving her. It was obvious to him that she liked him, possibly even fancied him. If he'd read the signals correctly, they could end up spending the night together. Is that what he wanted? She was hard to resist, especially looking so elegant and sophisticated in her bridesmaid's dress. He was tempted. There was too much temptation all around him today.

'So, everyone's gone,' said Scarlett looking at him with her frank green-eyed stare.

'Yes. It's just us.' And all the other guests who were lighting up the dance floor or sitting in dark corners getting drunk.

'What do we do now?' Scarlett asked, moving closer to him.

'Want do you want to do?'

'We could continue the party. Just the two of us?' Noah stiffened. There it was, the temptation. Scarlett was offering him the chance for them to spend the night together.

It would be so easy for him to say yes and for them to enjoy a delightful night. He had no doubt it would be delightful. She was gorgeous and he now knew that she wanted him. He was flattered and sorely tempted. He took a few seconds to imagine how it would be. Scarlett's red hair spread out on his pillow. *No, don't go there.* He had to say no. Reluctantly. But he had to be the strong one.

'I don't want you to do anything you'll regret tomorrow morning. Let me phone a taxi for you.'

Her demeanour changed in an instant. Dark red coloured her cheeks and she had tears in her eyes.

'Scarlett…' He held out his hand to her but she stood up and moved away. 'Wait, please let me explain.'

'No explanation necessary. I'll get my own taxi. Goodnight Noah.'

'Scarlett, don't be upset…' But she'd gone and he was left alone amongst the debris on the table. He had never wanted a drink more than he did at that moment.

CHAPTER TWELVE

M onday morning again and Scarlett wasn't in a good mood. How had she got it so wrong? She cringed when she thought of how she'd misread the signs from Noah. She thought he liked her, wanted to spend the night with her. She had made a fool of herself hinting that they should get together. What must he think of her? Now she had to go to work and act as if nothing had happened. Nothing had happened except her throwing herself at him.

But now it was back to business and Scarlett had been brought down to earth with a bump when she realised how much she had spent on the wedding and the dress and shoes for the hen night. When she checked her account online, she found she was in the red. Scarlett loathed being overdrawn, it made her feel a failure somehow.

Scarlett and Maria had used their savings to buy Esme out when she moved in with Joel. They had assured her that they would get a lodger to pay the missing third of the mortgage and bills but had done nothing about it yet. Maria hated the thought of a stranger living with them, but both of them were now struggling financially and something had to be done soon.

Noah was in his office when she arrived at work. She knocked on the door and opened it cautiously. He was sitting at his desk staring at the computer screen.

'Hi,' she said.

'Come in, Scarlett,' Noah said,' I've been reading Celine's notes and she's not doing as well as I'd like. We need to get her talking about her life and the main issues she's facing. Could you see if you can get her to open up a bit more?'

'Yes, of course.' Scarlett came into the room and stood next to his desk. Should she say something about the wedding? Or would it be better to keep quiet?

'Thanks. I'll see her later this morning.' Noah fiddled with a pen as he sat back in his chair. Perhaps he was eager to get back to work and she was preventing him.

'Right then, I'll leave you in peace.' He was still her boss after all. Maybe she should take her lead from him. This was a completely new situation for her. She turned to leave. Then turned back.

'Noah?'

'Yes?'

'Are you doing anything this weekend?' She cringed, hoping he didn't think she was propositioning him again.

'No, I've got no plans at all.' Noah was tapping his pen on the desk in a restless way. He obviously wanted to get back to work.

'I wondered if you'd like me to come round and show you what we need to do in the garden.'

He nodded. 'Okay. Saturday would be fine if that's okay with you.' He was making the effort to act normally so she would follow his lead. Perhaps he'd put her behaviour down to the champagne. He was watching her face as she stood next to his desk nervously twisting her fingers.

'Yes, fine. Okay then.'

'Good. See you later.' She was being dismissed and she almost ran out of the office. She needed to get over herself. Noah had obviously chosen to ignore her behaviour so she should too. Just carry on as normal. Whatever normal was.

Scarlett joined the team for the morning briefing. Miranda looked as gorgeous as ever. She wore a short summer dress and a cropped cardigan. She didn't look her usual cheerful self and after the briefing Scarlett went over to talk to her. When she saw her coming, her expression changed to a big smile as if she didn't have a care in the world.

'Hi, Scarlett. How was the wedding? Did it all go to plan? I love a wedding, don't you? Who caught the bouquet?'

'Um… I did actually.' That was the last thing she wanted to talk about. She'd been having a lovely conversation with Noah. It all went downhill after she caught the stupid bouquet.

'Really? No way! So you're next to get married. Do you have anyone in mind?'

'No. Not sure I want to get married. How about you? Did you have a good weekend?'

Miranda folded her arms and scowled. 'No, it was awful. I had a massive row with my flatmate. She's such a bitch. Told me to go out for the whole weekend as she has a new boyfriend and she's trying to impress him and didn't want me cluttering up the place.'

'That's awful, what did you do?'

'Stayed with my sister. Single mother with three kids. She expected me to look after them while she went out.' A single mother with three kids probably didn't get much chance to go out. Scarlett didn't say anything. It was none of her business.

'Why don't you move out?'

'Can't afford it. I don't like being on my own anyway. So… if you hear of anyone who wants a flat share or a lodger, let me know.'

'Sure. Will do.' Could she and Miranda live together and work together? Scarlett didn't find the idea appealing and she had one other person in mind to ask. She would keep Miranda as a last resort.

Noah wasn't proud of the fact that he'd upset Scarlett at the wedding reception. She hadn't deserved that. But she'd caught him off guard and he'd said the wrong thing. Totally made a mess of things.

Fortunately, the next time they'd met, they'd been civil with each other. They could be friends without anyone getting hurt. It was up to him to make sure he didn't send Scarlett any more mixed messages.

The doorbell rang, pulling him out of his musings.

'Scarlett, hi, come in.'

'Thanks.'

She was dressed ready for gardening in old blue jeans and a long-sleeved T-shirt. She wore no make-up and had pulled her hair up into a messy bun. Despite the fact that she had dressed down, Noah thought she looked gorgeous. The red-blooded male in him had appreciated the sexy look of the short, tight, green dress she had worn on the stag night, and the more mature man had found her ravishing in her maid of honour dress, but her natural look was the one he loved the best.

Women wore too much make-up in his opinion. A natural beauty like Scarlett didn't need any artificial trappings to enhance their looks. They just needed to be themselves.

He shouldn't be thinking of Scarlett like this. She was a work colleague and a friend. It was up to him to keep things platonic. What she wore and how she looked wasn't his concern.

Scarlett hovered in the hallway as if she wasn't sure of her welcome. Had he hurt her that much with his rejection of her because that was how she had viewed it? He hadn't meant it that way. Nothing would have made him happier than continuing the party with Scarlett, but that wasn't the right thing to do, much as it pained him to say so.

'Do you want a coffee before we start?' he asked.

'Could I have tea?'

'Of course, you can have what you want.' He smiled but she wasn't looking at him. She looked solemn, not a bit like the Scarlett he knew.

He busied himself with making the tea as Scarlett went outside to look at the garden. He watched her through the kitchen window. She looked tired, and beaten, and his heart went out to her. He knew how that felt but hated the thought that he had contributed to it.

She was looking closely at the flower beds. The sun shining on her hair highlighted the copper and gold strands. She seemed lost in her own private world. He watched her as she reached out and gently stroked the petals of a rose. Was she thinking of the wedding reception when she had absent-mindedly picked the petals off the rose in her bouquet? Had she already planned to ask him to spend the night with her? He had let her down by saying no. If he'd said yes, he would have let her down even more. He sighed heavily. Sometimes you just can't win.

When the tea was made, he carried the mugs outside, put them on the table on the patio then went back for some biscuits.

'Lovely day for gardening,' he said.

'Yes.'

'Scarlett? Are we okay? I'd hate to think you're still upset with me about what happened at the wedding.'

She sighed. 'No, I'm angry at myself. I threw myself at you. I'd drunk too much champagne. I don't have any excuse for my behaviour but that.' She stared at the table and hadn't eaten any of the biscuits which was a bad sign.

'You didn't throw yourself at me and I was flattered, really. You're beautiful—'

'You don't have to say that, it's okay.' Still she hadn't looked at him.

'I'm not just saying it, I really mean it. I think you're amazing, and gorgeous—'

'But not enough to... you know.'

He drank some of his tea and thought how to answer without upsetting her further. 'You told me you've never been in love, right. You deserve to be and you will be when you meet the right man. I'm not the right man because I don't want the same things you want—'

'How do you know what I want? I'm not even sure myself. Anyway, I wasn't asking you to marry me, just... maybe one night. And see where it led.' Scarlett stared at the garden, not meeting his eyes.

'The honest truth, Scarlett, is that I didn't take you up on the offer not because I don't fancy you, but because I do. You're an amazing woman and if things were different...' He let the sentence trail off, wondering how he would really feel if things had been different. 'I let someone down badly once—I'm not going into the details, not today—but it made me realise that I can't have anyone depending on me again in case I let them down too. Do you understand?'

'No. You'll have to be more specific.' Scarlett took a biscuit and dunked it in her tea. He smiled to himself. She was getting her old spirit back.

'Not today. I want us to be friends and for you to show me what to do in this amazing garden of Esme's.'

'Okay. Then let's get to work and stop idling around drinking tea.' She got up and wandered down to the shed at the bottom of the garden. He watched her, then drained his mug, and got up to follow her.

Soon they were both kneeling on proper garden kneelers that protected their clothes and had a pouch affair at the end to put the garden tools in.

'Joel told me he nearly ordered a pink one for Esme but chickened out and bought green,' said Noah.

'I'm glad he didn't. Esme hates pink.'

'I wonder how they're getting on in Tuscany.' Stick to the mundane, that was best. He'd steer away from anything more intimate.

'I bet they're having the time of their lives,' said Scarlett, sounding wistful. A couple of weeks in Italy sounded good to him too.

'Is that a weed?' asked Noah, reluctant to pull up anything he didn't recognise.

'Yep, well spotted.' Scarlett sounded as if she was back to normal and Noah was glad they'd had their little chat.

After about an hour they'd done one side of the garden and Noah had to admit it looked a lot tidier.

'What do you say to stopping for now and we'll finish the rest later in the week? Would you like to stay for dinner?' He hoped she said yes as he was enjoying being alone with her. He'd even enjoyed the weeding.

'Okay thanks. What are we having?' Scarlett packed away the gardening tools and started walking to the shed.

'Spaghetti Bolognese. Esme made the sauce so all I need to do is cook the pasta and even I can manage that. With garlic bread of course,' he called after her.

'Oh, well if there's garlic bread how can I refuse? Do you need any help?'

'No, I got it.' Scarlett opened the shed door and he want back into the house. He was pleased that they were friends again. Just keep it that way, he told himself.

Half an hour later, they sat down to the meal.

'This is lovely, Noah.'

'You can thank your sister for that.' He couldn't take any credit as he'd boiled water and warmed up garlic bread. Not exactly highly skilled.

'I've been thinking.' She spoke slowly and didn't look at him. Noah wondered what was coming next.

'Should I be worried?' he asked with a grin.

'We need someone to take Esme's place as we can't manage on our own. And you want to move out as soon as possible to let the newlyweds have some privacy, so… I wondered if we couldn't help each other out.'

'You're asking me to come and live with you and Maria?' His heart dropped to his boots when he realised he'd have to let Scarlett down again. But the only answer he could give her was no. It wouldn't work.

'It's just a suggestion. I'm sure we could make it work. After all, we're all adults and…' She trailed off and Noah felt bad for her.

'It's a lovely thought, really. But I'm not the easiest person to live with.'

'But you've been fine with Esme and Joel haven't you?' He could hear the disappointment in her voice and wondered what he could say that would convince her without hurting her.

'Yes, but I am looking forward to getting my own place again,' he lied. 'How about Miranda? I've heard she's looking for a house share?'

'Yes, I'll ask her.' She didn't seem happy about the prospect. But at least he was off the hook.

CHAPTER THIRTEEN

S carlett was pleased to see that Miranda was settling into the
ward well and seemed to be having more success than anyone
else in getting through to Celine. She had stopped saying she would
only speak to Noah and now included Miranda. The new nurse was
proving to be an asset to the team.

At the weekly team meeting, Noah was heaping praise on Miranda who was taking it all in her stride.

'You've done a great job in getting through to her,' Noah said,
'and you are to be congratulated. Well done.'

Scarlett had tried to talk to Celine, as Noah had requested, but
she had refused to speak to her. She couldn't help feeling she'd failed
where Miranda had succeeded but told herself that the patient was
the only person who mattered and her recovery was paramount.

There was a murmuring from the rest of the team and a few
smiles. It was unusual for Noah to single one person out for praise
as he believed it was always a team effort. Scarlett conceded that
Miranda deserved praise. After all she was new to the team.

'I think Celine is suffering from loneliness as well as alcohol addiction. If we could help her with that, it would be a big step forward.' Miranda looked around the group as she spoke.

'What about her fixation on Marilyn Monroe and the parallels she sees with her own life? Don't you think we should try to convince her that she isn't Marilyn and show her that she has control of her life; she isn't going to end up the same way as Marilyn did?'

Scarlett was more concerned with the risk of suicide attempts than her problem with alcohol.

'I don't know about that,' said Miranda, 'she hasn't mentioned anything to me. I think she's making real progress and we need to build on that.'

'Absolutely,' said Noah, 'but Scarlett is right, we need to address all the problems in Celine's life. We've got a long way to go yet, but everyone is doing a great job, so keep it up.'

They quickly concluded and dispersed. Scarlett stayed back to have a word with Miranda.

'Maria and I are looking for someone to share our house now that Esme's moved out. I didn't say anything before because I wanted to check with my sister.'

'Really? Oh, that's wonderful! What good timing.' Miranda grinned and clapped her hands in delight.

'You'll have to come and meet Maria and see the house of course. And if Maria wasn't happy or if you didn't like the house, then—'

'Oh, don't you worry about that. I'll love the house, especially after living in a cramped flat all those months. And I'm sure Maria and I will get on. When can I come and see it?' Scarlett hadn't thought Miranda would be so enthusiastic and had caught her off guard.

'Umm… tonight?'

'Shall I come home with you? That would be best, wouldn't it? Then I'll go back to the flat, pack my things and tell that miserable cow what I think of her.'

'Right. See you later then.' Scarlett had a sinking feeling in her stomach. Was she doing the right thing? After all, she didn't really know Miranda.

'Oh, thank you, I'm so happy. You really don't know what this means to me.' Miranda danced out of the room, leaving Scarlett alone with her thoughts.

She'd been disappointed when Noah turned down the offer to live with them. But not surprised. It had been a long shot born out of her desire to get closer to him. You never really knew someone until you lived with them, and the prospect of sharing a home with Noah had pushed her into all kinds of fantasies. Her favourite was how she'd accidently bump into him coming out of the bathroom dressed in only a skimpy towel. She needed to rein in her fertile imagination and get real. And the reality was that they needed money and Miranda needed a place to live.

If Maria didn't like her, she wouldn't be moving in. Should she have asked for references? Maybe they could give her a trial. Three months would be enough time to see if they could all live together in peace and harmony. And if there were any problems, she'd be out.

Scarlett drove Miranda home. They chatted amiably about this and that. Nothing of any importance. Miranda told her again how grateful she was, which made Scarlett feel bad. There was something about Miranda that she couldn't pin down. In some ways she was like a little girl, giggly and excitable. But she was a grown woman and a competent mental health nurse. She'd proved her worth in the unit and all the staff got on well with her.

And then there was Noah. She had told Scarlett she thought Noah was good looking, which of course he was, but did that mean that she had designs on him? Or was she jumping to conclusions? She was a natural flirt but she appeared to like Noah especially. At that thought Scarlett's hands gripped the steering wheel tightly and she found she was grinding her teeth. She forced herself to relax.

When they arrived, Maria was cooking a vegetable stir fry, one of her favourite meals. Delicious aromas filled the kitchen.

'What a gorgeous house! I love it! Do you own it yourselves?'

'Yes, the three of us bought it and Maria and I are paying the mortgage between us which is why we need a third.'

Scarlett wished they could cope with the mortgage on their own but neither of them had high paying jobs.

'Miranda, this is my sister, Maria. Maria, Miranda.'

'Hi,' Maria said smiling shyly.

'Hi Maria, that smells delicious. Do you do a lot of cooking?'

'No, we take it in turns.'

'Good. So I'll get the chance to cook for you.' Miranda beamed as if the idea excited her.

'Do you like cooking, Miranda?' Scarlett asked her. She didn't know much about the woman as they hardly ever talked about anything unconnected with work.

'I love cooking. I'm a foodie and, if I say so myself, am a bit of a cordon bleu cook.'

'Would you like to stay for dinner?' Maria asked.

What? Why was Maria asking her to stay for dinner? They'd never get rid of her. But maybe it was a good move. They could ask more questions and dig a bit deeper into her background. Maybe this could work after all. It would solve so many problems.

'I'd love to stay for dinner, that is so kind of you.'

'I'll show you the garden whilst we're here.' She opened the back door and Miranda poked her head out but said nothing. 'Do you like gardening?' Their garden wasn't as beautiful as Esme's but Scarlett was doing her best with it and would welcome some help.

'I've never had a garden but I'm willing to learn.'

'Would you like to see upstairs?' asked Scarlett. Of course she would. Stupid question. She'd never lived with a stranger before and didn't know how to behave.

'Yes, please!'

Maria had taken the box room for her bedroom as they had gone by seniority when they had bought the house. Esme had the biggest room, then Scarlett with Maria getting the short straw and the smallest bedroom. In true Maria fashion, she didn't seem to mind. If the people in her life were happy, Maria was too. She was the most selfless person Scarlett had ever known.

But a new lodger was a good opportunity to promote Maria to a bigger bedroom. It meant Miranda would have to make do with a tiny room and that might just be enough to persuade her not to accept. Did she want Miranda to take up the offer or didn't she?

Miranda, however, was one step ahead of her and made a beeline for Esme's old room even though the door was shut. She had a nerve, thought Scarlett.

'Is this my room? Oh, it's perfect. So spacious and with a lovely view of the front. Shame it doesn't look onto the garden. Great garden, by the way. Do you get a man in to do it for you? Do you sunbathe out there on the lawn? You know what would make that garden better? Decking and a hot tub. Trust me, my last place had one and we were never out of it. So, when can I move in?' Miranda bounced up and down on the bed which annoyed Scarlett. So bad mannered. But Miranda did think it was going to be her bed, so perhaps she could be excused. She needed to stop finding fault with everything Miranda did. They needed a third and she would be as good as anyone else.

'Maria and I will need to discuss it. I'll let you know in a few days.'

'Oh. Okay.'

Miranda looked disappointed but Scarlett was determined not to rush into anything. It was a big decision finding someone to share your home with. Not to be undertaken lightly. Now where had she heard that recently? Then she remembered—the wedding ceremony. An image of Noah looking up at her after she had propositioned him sent waves of embarrassment through her. She almost collapsed on the bed but willed herself to remain upright.

'I need to discuss it with my sister. And we'll need references from your last flat share.' That will slow her down. She was doing it again. *Get over yourself.*

'I understand. I can see you're a person who wants to do everything by the book and that's fine. No problem. I'll wait.'

'You won't have to wait too long.' She was beginning to feel guilty at dragging it out.

'Take all the time you need and I'll get those references for you.'

Thanks. I'd appreciate that.' Now she felt like the bad guy. 'Let's go and have dinner and we can talk some more.'

Miranda followed her down the stairs to the kitchen.

She asked for wine with her meal. Scarlett explained they only had wine on the weekend. It was a habit they'd begun when Esme had lived with them and anyway, Maria didn't drink.

'You don't drink any alcohol at all? Whyever not?'

'Because I don't like the taste,' said Maria calmly.

'How strange! I love a glass of wine with my meal, it's so civilised.'

Scarlett had finished her meal and Maria was on her last mouthful. Miranda was still eating. She ate carefully, chewing every mouthful umpteen times over, but she did finish what was on her plate.

'That was delicious, thank you Maria,' Miranda said.

'What kind of food do you like to eat, Miranda?' asked Scarlett.

'I can eat anything, I'm not a faddy eater. But I am watching my weight, so maybe a smaller portion next time. But it was delicious.'

'Okay.' Maria didn't seem phased by the woman's comments. Scarlett was though. Fancy insinuating that their portion sizes were too big. Was she calling them fat? What else was she going to criticise?

'I hope you don't mind but I'm going out tonight so I think I should go now.' Miranda smiled at them and Maria responded. Scarlett felt annoyed but she couldn't really say why. After all, Miranda hadn't said anything wrong, she just got on her nerves which wasn't a good start to their relationship.

'Do you want a lift anywhere?' asked Scarlett conscious of the fact that she had brought Miranda here from the hospital.

'Oh no, it's fine. I'll just ring for a taxi.' She ordered her transport while Maria and Scarlett washed up. When she got a text message to say the taxi was outside, she became effusive again and gushed her thanks and especially for the lovely meal.

'See you at work tomorrow,' said Scarlett.

'You will. See you later, Maria, it was lovely to meet you!' Miranda smiled her thousand-watt smile and waved at them.

As soon as the front door slammed, they both collapsed onto kitchen chairs and heaved heavy sighs.

'So, what do we think?' Scarlett filled the kettle and switched it on, then put teabags in the pot.

'She was okay. A bit over the top, but… beggars can't be choosers.'

'Are we beggars?' Scarlett poured the boiling water onto the teabags.

'I've been overdrawn since Esme left. I can't afford to pay half the mortgage, it's too much.'

'I'm so sorry, Maria. I didn't know it was that bad.' That's because she hadn't asked. Scarlett felt a wave of shame that she hadn't even thought of how Maria was coping. Her salary was less than Scarlett's, and the poor girl hardly ever went out.

'I didn't want to worry you.'

'Right, here's what we'll do. Tell Miranda she can have the room but there's a month's deposit and one month in advance.'

Scarlett poured the tea into two mugs, then added oat milk to both. Maria had asked her to try it as she wouldn't drink cow's milk anymore and Scarlett preferred it's creamy taste. Miranda would have to get to like it too or buy her own cow's milk.

'That might put her off.'

'It shouldn't. It's how most landlords operate. And if it does, we'll look for someone else. Do you think you can live with her?'

Maria shrugged. 'Yes, I suppose.'

'That wasn't very convincing,' said Scarlett.

'I can't really answer the question as I don't know her well enough. Living with someone is different to meeting them for an hour or so.'

'Good point. We need the money. We'll tell her it's a three months' trial.'

'Okay.'

'I'll tell her tomorrow.'

CHAPTER FOURTEEN

T he following day Miranda was waiting for Scarlett as she arrived on the ward.

'Scarlett, good morning. I know you said a few days and I don't want to mither you but, have you by any chance made a decision? I love your house and I think we'll all get on well.'

Scarlett wanted to start her day looking after the patients, but this needed sorting out first. She took Miranda into the staff office.

'Okay, here's the deal. We'll need a deposit of a month's rent, plus the first month's rent in advance. You can move in the weekend after next. Do you need any help moving your things?'

'Is there no chance I could move in earlier?' Miranda asked, 'My lease is coming to an end and I'd really like to be settled in my next place as soon as I can. You understand don't you?' Miranda's big blue eyes were pleading and Scarlett realised how desperate she was to move out.

'Don't you need to give your present landlord some notice?' Scarlett scrambled to think of some delaying tactics. But she was only delaying the inevitable.

'Oh don't worry about her. It serves her right if I just left. No, it'll be fine. I really need to get away from there, it's affecting my mental health.'

'I'm sorry to hear that. What about the money? Is it acceptable?' It's a lot of money so she might say no.

Miranda waved the question away. 'Oh sure, not a problem. Could I move in tomorrow night?' She smiled hopefully.

'So soon?' Scarlett wasn't expecting that, but at least they'd have some money to help with the bills.

'I really need to move out of my present place before I go crazy.' She laughed. What had happened to her that was so bad it was affecting her mental health?

'Okay. I'll give you a set of keys when you've moved in. We'll both be at home tomorrow.'

'Thank you so much, you don't know what this means to me.'

'Well… I hope you'll be happy with us.' Scarlett had serious doubts they'd be happy with her, but she'd said yes now, there was no backing down.

'Oh I will, I just know I will.'

The following evening, Scarlett and Maria were watching TV and waiting for the doorbell to ring.

Maria was relaxed and absorbed in watching Bake-Off. Scarlett couldn't rest and fidgeted, getting up and peering out of the window, before throwing herself back down into the armchair.

When the doorbell finally rang, she jumped up and went to answer it, closely followed by Maria.

A large van had pulled up outside. What the…?! Surely she hadn't brought furniture with her. There was no room in their house for any more and she didn't need it. Scarlett felt sick. Why had she agreed to Miranda staying with them?

'Hi, I'm here!' she shouted as she scrambled out of the passenger side.

'So I see,' Scarlett muttered darkly. She forced herself to smile as Miranda skipped up the path.

'Don't worry about the size of the van,' Miranda said laughing, 'My friend has kindly agreed to bring my stuff in his furniture van. It's not full, I promise.'

'Thank goodness for that,' she said to Maria. 'Come on, we better go and help her.'

They joined Miranda as the friend opened the doors and they were speechless at the sight of six metal clothes racks, packed with dresses, skirts, tops, trousers. Had she raided Harvey Nichols on the way here?

The friend took one end and Miranda took the other. They pushed the racks to the platform at the end of the van and the friend pulled a lever to lower the platform to ground level.

'Our turn,' said Scarlett to Maria as they copied the action after bringing the platform up to van level.

'This is fun,' said Maria as the platform lowered.

'I worry about you sometimes. If this is your idea of fun, you are definitely not getting out enough.'

'How are we going to get the racks up the stairs?' asked Maria.

'Maybe friend will help Miranda. I don't see why we should do any of the donkey work, do you?' Why did she have so many clothes? And where would they put them? If she thought any of them were going in her bedroom she was mistaken. Miranda was getting the biggest room so shouldn't expect any more concessions.

'It'd be a nice gesture. She can't do it all alone.' Maria was right. They should help.

When the racks had been taken out of the van and were sitting in the garden and the hallway, the friend couldn't get away fast enough. They'd have to do it all themselves.

'Why don't you take the clothes up and put them on the bed and then we can carry the racks up empty? They're too heavy to take upstairs laden as they are now,' Scarlett suggested.

'Yes, I suppose you're right. I might invest in another wardrobe. There'll be enough room in the bedroom if I move things around a bit,' Miranda said thoughtfully.

Scarlett sighed and Maria gave her a quick hug while Miranda was looking the other way.

Two hours later, the clothes and racks had been moved into the front bedroom. The room, that had looked neat and tidy, looked a mess with clothes everywhere and the metal racks were very much in the way. But that was Miranda's problem, she had seen the size of the bedroom and should have decluttered her wardrobe before she moved in.

Maria made tea and they sipped it, listening to the sounds of Miranda stomping about upstairs.

'Have you ever had the feeling you've made a terrible mistake?' Scarlett asked Maria. She had hoped Miranda would have given them the money upfront, but so far it hadn't been mentioned.

'Is that how you're feeling now?' Scarlett nodded. 'Give her a chance. It's hard to move into a house with two sisters or two friends. She must feel as if she's the odd one out. We need to try and make her feel welcome. Don't you think?'

'As always, you're right. I'll do my best, but I'm not promising anything.'

Noah needed a break and escaped to the relative safety of the hospital dining room. No one bothered him there and he could have his ten minute lunch break in peace and quiet. Usually. Today, however, Miranda must have followed him for no sooner had he sat down to eat his cheese and tomato sandwich and drink a glass of water, than she sat opposite him.

'Hi,' Miranda gushed, 'I just wanted to let you know that I've moved in with Scarlett and her sister. Isn't that cool?'

'Yes, very cool. Good for you.'

'I knew you'd be happy for me. You're such a kind man, concerned with your staff's welfare as well as the patients.'

'Well... thanks.' Noah never knew what to say when complimented. He squirmed with embarrassment. 'How are you settling into the job? Any problems?'

'Oh no, none at all, I'm having a great time. In fact, I was wondering if you wanted to come out for a drink one night. To celebrate. Things haven't been easy recently and now they're starting to improve and it's mainly down to you.'

'Me?' How the heck could it be down to him? He hadn't done anything.

'Yes, you. You don't realise what a good person you are. I think we should get to know each other better. Outside work I mean. We could be good for each other.'

'I'm flattered. Truly. But I'm not sure that would be such a good idea. But thanks for being so honest.' Noah had already had fifteen minutes break and needed to get back to work. But Miranda was gazing at him with come-to-bed eyes and he felt unable to stand up.

'Think about what I've said, Noah. No strings. Just a bit of fun.'

Then she stood up and left. He watched her as she strolled out of the dining-room, smiling at those who smiled at her first. Mainly men.

What did he do? He liked Miranda and she was a good nurse. He had a lot of respect for her and was happy that her life had improved by coming to work in the unit. But that was as far as it went. She didn't cause his heart to beat faster, or his breath to quicken. Not like another nurse who shall be nameless. That one did strange things to his mind. Just the sound of her voice and the depth of her green eyes—eyes he could drown in—made him forget everything but the beautiful woman in front of him. Or not in front of him. He could conjure her image and imagine them together.

But he mustn't think like that. For his peace of mind, which had deserted him the moment Miranda sat down, he needed to stop thinking of both of them. Lose himself in work. Helping people like Celine. Forget the past no matter how impossible that seemed and live in the moment. Easy to say, difficult to do. But he owed it to his patients. They were all that mattered now.

Scarlett had kindly offered to help Noah clean the house and make sure it was up to Esme's high standards for the happy couple's return that afternoon.

'Scarlett, hi, come in. Thanks for this, I appreciate it.'

'No problem,' she said. 'Shall we get stuck in and stop for a rest when we've done the cleaning?'

'Sounds like a plan.' He smiled but Scarlett had already headed to the kitchen.

They dusted, hoovered, cleaned the kitchen and bathroom then washed the floors. Scarlett made a chicken casserole while Noah helped by chopping vegetables.

'How's Miranda settling in?' Noah had been pleased when Miranda had told him she was going to be the McBride sisters' new lodger, seeing as how he'd been the one to suggest it. He hoped they'd get on.

'Okay. She has half a department store complete with clothes racks in her bedroom and a suitcase full of make-up, but that's her problem, it's not going to overflow to the rest of the house.'

No wonder Scarlett sounded irritable. It can't be easy living with a stranger, especially a high maintenance one like Miranda.

'Give her time. It's not easy living with strangers. You need to get used to each other and lay down some ground rules.'

'You sound as if you speak from experience. Have you shared with strangers?' Scarlett looked up from preparing the casserole.

'Not since I was a medical student.' He had backed himself into a corner. Those days were full of painful memories and he really didn't want to talk about it. Hopefully Scarlett wouldn't question him. They had all been strangers when they started their medical training but soon became friends, united in the stress they were all under.

'Noah? How did you know Miranda had moved in with us?' Scarlett frowned as she waited for his reply.

'She told me. We had lunch together recently as she had a few things she wanted to discuss.' Not a total lie. He was getting used to being economical with the truth where Miranda was concerned.

'She's very attractive, isn't she? In fact, she's beautiful.' She sipped her tea. Then picked up the peeler to finish peeling the carrots. He was obviously taking too long.

'Yes, I suppose she is. What of it?' Noah sensed danger. Did Scarlett feel threatened by her?

'I just mean most men wouldn't be able to resist her. She's quite stunning.'

'I'm not most men.' Is that what was bothering her? Did she think he fancied Miranda?

'No… but if you wanted to go out with her I wouldn't blame you.' Scarlett couldn't look him in the eye, she concentrated hard on peeling the carrots.

'I don't.'

'Why not?'

Because she's not a redhead with green eyes that shine like emer-alds. 'I just don't. I don't want to go out with every attractive woman I meet.'

'You don't? Do you prefer the ugly ones?' He threw back his head and laughed. That was more like the Scarlett he knew and loved. Why had he used the L word? He glanced at her to find her watching him. He wondered what she was thinking.

They heard a key in the lock. Esme and Joel were home.

CHAPTER FIFTEEN

'If you're not busy on Friday night, Noah, put on your dancing shoes… we're going to Latin Nights,' said Scarlett.

Noah was at his computer frowning at an email he was trying to compose. She probably shouldn't be disturbing him like this at work but she was excited and wasn't going to take no for an answer. She longed to dance with him again, to experience the feeling they'd both had at the wedding reception. It had been electric but this time she wouldn't ruin it by propositioning him. Although her whole being longed to experience it again, even if it didn't lead anywhere.

'Latin Nights?' he asked, leaning back in his chair.

'It's a salsa club that's recently opened. I'm getting a group together. The first half of the evening is a lesson, then the rest of the time it's a free for all. Please say you'll come. Esme and Joel are going.'

'Have you asked them? They haven't mentioned it to me.'

'Not yet, but I know they will. They love dancing. Go on, let your hair down.'

'What night?' He obviously hadn't been listening when she first came in as she'd already told him it was Friday.

'Every Friday night. It'll be fun.' Noah watched her with a guarded look. He was so hard to read sometimes.

Scarlett was finding it more difficult to persuade him than she thought. He hadn't said no, or yes. In fact he just sat there watching her. She did a few turns and moved her hips in the way she presumed salsa dancers did, while humming the theme tune from Strictly. He smiled at her. Then grinned broadly. That's better.

'What's going on in here?' She hadn't heard the door open and Miranda come in. The grin wasn't for herself, it was for Miranda. 'Am I interrupting something?'

'No, nothing…' Scarlett said.

'Scarlett was just trying to get me to go dancing with her.' Noah grinned broadly.

'Not just me… a group of us.' She felt embarrassed now as if he was laughing at her. 'A salsa club is starting salsa lessons on Friday nights. I'm trying to get people to come with me.' Why had she said it like that? It made her sound like billy-no-mates having to beg people to go out with her.

'What do you think, Noah? Shall we go?' Miranda said.

'Okay, I give in. Put my name down.' Noah turned back to his computer. 'Now if there's nothing else, we should all really get back to work.'

'Right. I'll put your names down then.' Noah was already absorbed in the email he was typing and didn't reply.

As they headed back to the ward, Scarlett wondered what Miranda had wanted with Noah. Nothing important, obviously.

Latin Nights was decorated in bright colours; lots of hot red and yellow. There were posters all around the walls. Some were advertising coming events with the silhouette of couples in tango, samba and salsa moves. Salsa music played quietly in the background.

Scarlett and Miranda had arrived first and were waiting for the rest of the group. Maria had opted out, saying it wasn't her thing. She was happy curled up on the couch watching Gogglebox.

Scarlett had chosen a soft drink and Miranda was drinking white wine. She wished the others would hurry up and arrive as she had no idea what to say to Miranda. She really needed to make the effort though.

Since Miranda had moved in, they'd seen little of each other. Their lodger seemed to like being out. She hadn't paid them any money yet, which was something that needed correcting soon. She'd give her a few days more before mentioning it.

'Have you done salsa before?' A bit of a lame question but better than sitting in silence. Scarlett wasn't like Esme and Maria, who never spoke unless they had something to say. She could witter for England.

'Yes, of course. Who hasn't these days?' Scarlett hadn't for a start.

Scarlett felt relieved when the rest of the group turned up.

When the introductions had been made and everyone had drinks, Scarlett sidled up to Noah.

'I'm looking forward to this. Aren't you?' She decided she liked seeing Noah in casual clothes. He looked younger in blue jeans and a T-shirt. The sharp citrus smell of his after shave washed over her playing havoc with her erogenous zones. She breathed in deeply, trying to commit the scent to memory.

'I am but I'm a bit nervous too. From what I've seen of your family, the McBrides take to dancing like ducks to water. Not so the Whittaker's. I think we've all got two left feet.'

Scarlett remembered his skill on the dance floor at the wedding reception and was just about to argue, when the salsa teacher, whose name was Anton, requested the beginners to follow him.

They all piled on to the dance floor and stood in rows in front of him. Scarlett stood at the front so she could watch Anton's feet. She was hoping that Noah would stand next to her, but he moved to the end of the row instead.

Esme, who was already an expert at salsa dancing, and Miranda, stood behind the group as they didn't need the instruction the beginners did.

Anton showed them some basic steps. How to move forward, back and then sideways. There was no music and some people found it hard to keep the beat. Scarlett picked it up quite quickly.

She glanced behind her. Miranda was now standing next to Noah and it was clear from the way she moved that she knew what she was doing. She wore a short dress that flared around her thighs and Scarlett felt the green eyed monster rear its ugly head. She was dressed in jeans and a T-shirt as she had few dresses and none suitable for a salsa class. There was only one thing for it, she'd learn this dance and become better than Miranda. Even if it meant having private lessons with Esme and practicing on her days off. And she'd buy some suitable dresses.

Her sister was dancing on her own at the back, her red dress making her look more of a Latin beauty than ever.

When they had to partner up, there was an odd number, so Anton—a slim but incredibly nimble man who looked as if he had been born doing the salsa—asked Esme if she would help him to demonstrate some more moves.

'Now, I want you to do the basic step, forward and back, then when I tell you, have a go at the side step and don't forget to move those hips. And, sorry ladies, the men lead, so you have to follow them.' There was a smattering of laughter.

'I'm Steve by the way,' said the man from the improvers group that Scarlett was partnered with.

'Scarlett,' she replied. 'You're good at this.' She was glad as following his lead was helping her learn the steps quickly. 'If I'd been partnered with a beginner like me we would both have ended up in the proverbial ditch.'

After a short while Scarlett was really getting into it and felt she could be good at salsa dancing. She had to keep reminding herself that this was just the first lesson. When she watched Esme dancing with Anton, she realised how much there was to learn.

The dampener on the evening was that Noah was dancing with Miranda. They looked as if they'd been dancing together all their lives. Maybe they had danced together before. Was she being naïve where those two were concerned? Were they secretly seeing each other? Noah had let slip that they'd had lunch together. He didn't normally have time for lunch. He'd never asked her to go to lunch with him.

'Right class, that was good. You've all done so well that I think we'll add just one more move and then let you go to enjoy the rest of the evening. Esme? Do you mind demonstrating a right turn?'

Esme didn't. She made it look so easy.

'Right guys, there's ten minutes left in the class, so I want you to get used to dancing with different partners. All the men move to your left, so you are partnering someone new.'

Scarlett found herself partnered with Derek, an elderly man with wet patches under his armpits.

The music started, Derek wiped his hands on his trousers and they got into hold. They managed to do the basic front and back, but Derek looked at her in shock when Anton called out that they should have a go at the turn. In the end, Scarlett turned herself, leaving Derek staring at her with his mouth open like a goldfish.

'Okay, move on again,' shouted Anton.

Her next partner had no rhythm and couldn't even master the most basic moves. She felt sorry for him as he had no idea what he was doing. He didn't speak, thank goodness, and Scarlett was relieved when the class finished.

If she'd learned one thing in the previous hour, it was that salsa was much more fun with a good dance partner.

Scarlett's only objective now was to dance with Noah. She watched carefully as Miranda dragged him onto the dance floor with the advanced group. The poor man didn't know what he was doing as Miranda was showing off, doing moves they hadn't been taught. She waited her chance. The woman must need the toilet at some point and then she'd be there.

After a while it was obvious that Miranda wasn't letting go of Noah. Sod this for a game of soldiers, she was going to be proactive.

She walked over and said, "Right, Miranda, I'm cutting in. Why don't you dance with someone else?'

'What?' Miranda stepped back and Scarlett took her place.

She moved into hold and stared at Noah daring him to make some facetious remark. He grinned at her and pulled her close to him. Not the hold you use for salsa but she wasn't complaining. When he moved her into the proper hold and held her hand, she felt intoxicated by his closeness. He still smelt divine, despite all the physical exertion they'd been doing. She caught the waft of his citrussy, spicy scent. She could think of a different type of exertion she wouldn't mind sharing with Noah but pushed the thought out of her mind.

'Are you enjoying yourself?' she asked Noah.

'I am now,' he said.

'Good. Shall we do it all again next week?' And the next week she was dancing with him right from the beginning.

'Yes, good idea. If I'm not busy at work.'

Someone had turned the music up and the beat thrummed through her lighting up her nerve endings. She waggled her hips and tried to look as sexy as possible. Noah watched her with a half-smile that softened his features. His eyes were dark and unfathomable.

They danced in silence, concentrating on getting the steps right. After a short while they moved together as one and Scarlett felt her spirits soar at the feeling of joy being close to him and moving together evoked. They were made to dance together. She couldn't believe she'd only been learning the salsa for a matter of hours. She was born for this. No wonder Esme loved it so much.

She stayed with Noah for the rest of the evening. She wasn't letting go of him for anyone.

CHAPTER SIXTEEN

Noah arrived at the hospital an hour earlier than usual. He hoped he could spend some of that time reading the emails and reports he needed to catch up on without women invading his office sitting on his desk and teasing him with dresses riding up their thighs or enticing him to join them in a salsa class.

He smiled when he thought of Scarlett and how sexy and uninhibited she seemed moving her hips and tossing her hair over her shoulder. She loved every minute of it and her joy was infectious. He enjoyed it too. It had been a long time since he'd been able to let himself go like that and throw himself into the dance. He'd definitely go back the following Friday. It would make a change from pounding the treadmill at the gym.

Miranda was a bit of a problem though. She hadn't been pleased when Scarlett had cut in when they were dancing, but he certainly had been. Miranda was a lovely woman, and yes… gorgeous looking, and it appeared she might be his for the taking. But it wasn't going to happen.

He liked Miranda as a work colleague and maybe a friend. But that was it. He had no feelings for her at all of a sexual nature. Whereas, when he was anywhere in Scarlett's orbit, his pulse raced and his throat dried up. Strange behaviour for a man rapidly approaching his thirty-sixth birthday. He wasn't sixteen any more for goodness sake.

Right. No more wool gathering. Back to work. He was anxious to see how Celine was getting on.

He walked to her room, knocked on the door and heard a bright and breezy "come in" from his patient. He went in.

'Hello, Celine, how are you today?'

'Noah, how lovely to see you.' Celine put her hand out to him as if she was at home and graciously welcoming a gentleman caller.

'You're looking well.' She was. Her complexion had improved, and she was a much better colour. The wan, pasty look had gone, and she was wearing expertly applied make-up. Her clothing was fashionable, and she had a wig that suited her, unlike the red monstrosity that she had sported before.

'I'm feeling well. I really don't know why I'm still here.'

'The good news, Celine, is that we are letting you go, with the proviso that you see someone on an outpatient basis. It doesn't have to be me, although I'd be delighted to see you of course, but we do feel that you would benefit from some support in the community.'

'So, you could still be my psychiatrist?'

'Of course, but I see my patients privately, not on the NHS.'

'That's fine, Noah. I would like to continue as your patient seeing as you know me so well and we have already formed a relationship of a kind, in a medical sense of course.'

'I'll let you settle back into the outside world and then you can tell me when you're ready to see me.'

'How about you give me your mobile number and then I can ring you when I'm ready to make an appointment?'

'We don't usually give our private numbers to patients. You can ring me here instead.'

'Oh, come now, Noah, I'm not any old patient am I? And it would make life so much easier if I could reach you direct.'

Noah thought about what she'd said. It would make life easier for both of them.

'Alright then.' He wrote his number on his business card and handed it to Celine. 'Don't give it to anyone else though, will you?'

'I wouldn't dream of it. I shall keep it all to myself.' She smiled and Noah was pleased at how much better she looked.

'Is there anything you want to ask me or talk about?'

'No. Thank you for everything you've done for me and it's good to know you're there if I need you. As a kind of safety net.'

'Good. Right. I'll get your discharge arranged. Best of luck with everything, Celine.' She blew him a kiss, but his thoughts were already on the next patient on his list.

Scarlett intended to confront Miranda about the money she still owed them. Maria was still in the red and Scarlett was dangerously close to it again.

Her house mate was in the kitchen baking and Maria was at Mum's.

'Hi, that smells good.'

'It's chocolate fudge cake and you'll love it. Wait 'til you taste it.'

'Great.' Did Miranda not realise that they were a baking family? Maybe she should introduce her to Candy Dots and the wonderful cakes, biscuits and pastries that Mum and Dot made every day. And all the McBride sisters could bake cakes with their eyes shut. Not that other people wouldn't be as good as they were; she accepted that she was biased.

'Is your sister home now with her new husband? That must feel so strange, mustn't it? To suddenly have a husband. I can't wait until I get married.'

'Have you got anyone in mind?' Scarlett couldn't resist asking the question even though she knew she was setting herself up for a fall. She sat at the kitchen table and watched Miranda stir a bowl of butter cream.

'Well…' she turned around and her blue eyes were shining, 'I rather do, but it's early days, so I'm not saying anything yet. I hope you understand. But I promise you'll be the first to know if I have any news.'

'Okay, thanks.' It was obvious she meant Noah. Who else could it be? She'd never mentioned a boyfriend, let alone a fiancé. A woman with her looks must have men running after her all the time. She probably had the pick of them.

'I need to ask you something Miranda, and it's a bit delicate.' Hopefully she'd guess what she was going to ask and save her the embarrassment of having to mention it.

'Okay, honey, fire away.' Miranda was absorbed in her buttercream and oblivious to anything else.

Scarlett sighed. 'It's about the money you owe. I'm really sorry, but we need it.'

Miranda came and sat down at the table and took Scarlett by the hand. 'I know, and I'm desperately embarrassed by this, but there's been a delay with the deposit on my last place. I'll get you the money, I promise. I haven't forgotten. Okay?' Miranda let go of her hand and patted it, before getting up and returning her attention to the buttercream.

Where did she go from here? Should she suggest that Miranda has a car boot sale and sells her six racks of clothes and umpteen pairs of shoes? That was where the money went—on clothes, shoes and make-up. And it wasn't as if she needed all the trappings to make her look attractive as some women did. Miranda had the kind of looks that were seen on the covers of fashion magazines. Not that she envied her. Although she did, a little. Okay, a lot. She wished she had her looks. But wishing never changed anything as her mum was always telling her. She had red hair and freckles and was stuck with it.

CHAPTER SEVENTEEN

Two days later Noah was in work early again but this time Miranda followed him into his office.

'Hi Noah,' she sang brightly, 'Good morning. How are you?'

'I'm fine thanks, how are you?'

'I'm good. But I want to ask you a favour.'

He plastered a smile on his face and tried to shrug off his irritation. Would he ever be allowed to get on with his work? 'What kind of favour?'

'I don't really want to talk about it here in case we're overheard. Anybody could walk in.' She looked over her shoulder as if she was checking for eavesdroppers. 'I know, let's go for a pizza after work and I'll tell you all about it.' She smiled seductively and Noah's heart sank. How could he say no without upsetting her? Should he say no? She was a colleague asking for his help. He had a duty of care to his staff so the least he could do was hear her out. He didn't want to let her down.

'Okay. About six?' He had to admit he was curious to hear what she wanted. Obviously if it was something he could help with, he would.

'Brilliant! Thanks ever so much. Bye.' She waggled her fingers at him in a cute way and he wondered what he had got himself into.

Pizza First was packed but they managed to get the last table for two in the window. Noah tried to ignore the people walking by who stared in at them. There were customers queuing at the counter as Pizza First had started out as a take-away business before they added tables and chairs. It was cheap and cheerful but the pizza was delicious.

'What are you having?' Noah asked Miranda.

'Well, I don't have a big appetite and could only eat a couple of slices. Would it be okay if we shared?'

'Fine. I'll just order a supreme.'

When the food arrived with a couple of soft drinks, Noah realised he was hungry and ate three slices to Miranda's one.

'So… what are you doing for your birthday?'

'I don't normally celebrate my birthday, but Esme pointed out that there's a Saturday Night Extravaganza at Latin Nights, so I might get a gang of us to go there.'

'Oh super! Who are you going to invite?' Miranda nibbled at her pizza slice and stared at him with wide eyes.

'Anyone who wants to come. All the McBrides of course and people from work. You would be most welcome to join us.'

'Oh thank you, I'd love to come. It must be lovely to be part of a big family like Scarlett is. I really envy her. Can I bring someone?'

'Of course you can.' Noah was surprised and wondered if she had a boyfriend they didn't know about. He hoped so.

'Umm, this is lovely,' she said. She'd eaten one piece. Noah had left three slices for her and he was still hungry.

'Another slice?'

'No, I'm full now. You have the rest.'

Noah got stuck in not needing to be told twice.

'Okay, now we've eaten, maybe you can tell me why we're here.' Did that come across as rude? Maybe. But she had said she needed a favour.

'It's a bit embarrassing but... I want an advance on my salary. I wouldn't ask if it wasn't important. I approached Human Resources but they said it wasn't usual protocol. I just wondered if there was anything you could do to help.' She looked at him with baby blue eyes and fluttered her eyelashes. She had obviously learned from a young age that to get what you want in life, you had to use the gifts nature had given you. And she used them to perfection.

'Sure, I can help but it depends on how much you need.'

'As much as I can get,' she laughed in a breathy way and smiled sweetly.

He sighed. 'The only problem with that is next month. If you get most of your salary now, how are you going to manage further down the line?'

'I'll have to sell my body.' She giggled and put the tip of her index finger in her mouth. 'Sorry that was a joke.'

Noah had realised for a while that the moves she made were studied, unnatural. They weren't the real Miranda. If only she could learn to be herself. She was a sweet girl when she wasn't playacting and could stop trying to impress people.

'Are you in trouble?'

'No. Not trouble. Okay, I'll tell you.' Miranda sighed and looked genuinely worried. 'I can't pay Scarlett the money I owe for the deposit and first month's rent. And I really like living there and don't want to have to move out.' She chewed on her lower lip and waited silently.

'How much?' She told him and he took his phone out of his pocket and logged on to the online banking app. 'Give me your bank details – sort code and account number.' Miranda looked at him hopefully. She gave him the information and he sent the money through. 'There, done.'

'Noah, I didn't mean for you to give me the money yourself.' She leaned over the table and spoke earnestly. There was no acting now, she was being herself.

'I know you didn't but this is the best way. You can start with a clean slate.'

'I really don't know how to thank you.' She smiled sadly. 'I knew you were a special man right from the first moment I saw you. I will pay you back, I promise.'

'No need.' He hoped they could change the subject now. All this talk of him being special made him cringe. He knew the truth. He was as far from special as it was possible to be.

Just as he was about to put his phone back in his pocket it rang. It was Celine.

'I need to get this.' He got up and went outside.

'Can I see you? I'm struggling.' Celine sounded drunk. Noah's heart sank.

'Okay. Meet me at my office in half an hour.'

Celine was drunk and tearful. She sat in a chair opposite him, hunched over and sobbing quietly. She was in a world of pain and her grief was genuine. He recognised the despair she must be feeling, from the rocking back and forwards with her arms wrapped around herself, to her tear-stained face and unkempt appearance.

Noah waited for her to be ready to talk. He didn't hurry her by asking questions. He wanted her to know he had all the time in the world and would wait for as long as it took. He was here to help her, not criticise, reprimand, or show any disappointment in her at all. He knew from personal experience that no one could make her feel worse than she already did. She was her own worst critic and his job was to listen, and then encourage her, tell her that it was just a small slip. She could get back to being teetotal again.

'You must hate me,' she said eventually. 'All the work you and your team did was all for nothing. It was different in the hospital. Everyone knew why I was there and they wanted to help. In the outside world, everyone is trying to get you to drink.'

Noah agreed with her. Which is why he did his utmost to stay away from places that sold alcohol. Celine would have to learn this for herself. It must be difficult, though, being in show business. The opportunities for drinking must be far worse than he had to deal with.

'No one hates you, Celine. We all still want you to kick the habit, and you will. It was one slip, that was all.'

'I was out for days. I don't even know how many.'

'Do you feel up to telling me about it?' He spoke gently, fully expecting her to say no.

'I went to a party. There was a woman there who was pregnant. She kept saying how happy she was and I couldn't bear it. I left and on the way home I called into the off licence. So many bottles to choose from. I bought a few. Wine, vodka, whisky…'

Celine started crying again. Quietly, tears rolling down her flushed cheeks. Noah waited without speaking.

Then she gasped, as if she'd been under water and had reached the surface suddenly. Then the keening started. A wailing that pierced his heart and made him want to jump up and put his arms around her. But that wasn't why he was there. He couldn't help but be moved by listening to Celine in so much pain. Maybe when it was over he'd tell her that showing vulnerability is a strength not a weakness, and crying can be a release. Toxins are released when we cry, self-soothing ones. Although not all therapists would agree. As a profession there were many opinions on patients' behaviour.

But he felt he knew Celine well now. Much better than he had when she was first admitted. She had opened up on the ward and on some of the group therapy sessions. He saw himself in her. He had gone through the same pain she was experiencing.

When the crying stopped, Noah waited for her to say something. She looked drained of all energy and hope. She was the picture of despair. Despite telling himself this was all about Celine, his thoughts drifted back to a time he'd done exactly the same thing. Gone on a drunken spree and lost a whole weekend.

'I'm pathetic, aren't I?' Celine said miserably.

'No, you're hurt and in pain. I know you probably don't believe this but things will get better. You're not alone, Celine and together we'll get you through this. I promise.'

CHAPTER EIGHTEEN

Scarlett dashed home to get changed and drive herself and Maria to Mum's. Noah, Joel and Esme would arrive a bit later.

'Have you seen the cake? What do you think? Will he like it?' Candy said nervously. She was obviously eager to impress Noah.

'Mum, he'll absolutely love it. He wasn't expecting any of this, he'll be made up.'

'Good. I hope so.'

Scarlett peeked at the cake. It was a medically themed fruit cake decorated in white fondant icing. A white coat contained a pair of scissors and a scalpel in the pockets, and a stethoscope curled on the top. It had "Happy Birthday Noah" in perfect writing and was a work of art.

'You know, Mum, I think you and Dot should start selling novelty cakes. You could charge a lot for them. People would love them.' Scarlett was so proud of her mum and the way she had taken running a business in her stride.

'I think we're going to see how the teas and coffees go down first before any more expansion of the business.'

The doorbell rang and Scarlett went to answer it. Esme, Joel and Noah had arrived.

'Happy birthday, Noah!' shouted Candy and Connie together.

'Now don't embarrass him,' said Joel with an evil grin which they all took to mean embarrass him all you like.

Scarlett gave him a quick kiss on the cheek. 'Happy Birthday,' she whispered. She felt a trembling inside at being so close to him. He looked happy if a bit self-conscious by all the attention.

They gave him presents of ties, after shave, chocolates and cards, mainly humorous ones.

Scarlett was last and watched his face closely as he stared at the envelope she thrust into his hands. She loved giving presents, in fact she enjoyed giving more than receiving and intended to make the most of his birthday to see his eyes light up with pleasure. She really hoped he understood the message she was trying to send.

Noah was examining the envelope which was plain white with nothing on it. He kept shooting her questioning looks with a smile dancing across his face as he saw how impatient she was getting.

He started to open the envelope. Scarlett's heart was in her mouth. What if he didn't like it? Maybe he wouldn't be interested…

When he finally took out the contents, he read it and did a double take. He stared at her without speaking, his mouth open and his eyes sparkling. 'You've done this for me?' Scarlett noticed his voice was husky and she swore his eyes were wet with tears. She couldn't have hoped for a better reaction. She grinned at him.

'What? What has she done for you?' asked Connie, trying to read the piece of paper that had been in the envelope. She wasn't the most patient person in the world.

'Is it a voucher?' asked Candy.

'Come on, Bro, don't keep us in suspense,' said Joel.

Noah handed the voucher to Joel who read it quickly. 'Wow! What a present. Well done, Scarlett.'

Noah walked slowly towards Scarlett and hugged her. He held her tenderly and Scarlett felt her own eyes tear up. She relaxed into his arms, feeling safe in his embrace. Cherished. She didn't want the hug to end.

'Thank you so much. That is the best thing anyone has ever given me,' he whispered.

'Okay, I'll have to read it then,' said Joel. 'Scarlett has gifted Noah with a voucher to enable him to... and I quote, 'hurtle around the racetrack at blistering speeds in two—yes not one but two—amazing supercars. The choice is: Ferrari, Aston Martin, Lamborghini or Porsche. And I know which one Noah will choose for the first. Not sure about the second. And that's not all. He then gets to be a passenger in the car that a real racing driver is going to make go a lot faster apparently.'

'Oh my, you speed freak,' said Connie looking at Noah admiringly. 'I didn't know you were a petrol head like my sister.'

'Is it safe?' asked Candy.

'Yes, Mum, perfectly safe,' said Scarlett.

'Well, to each their own I suppose. Right people, let's eat,' said Candy.

Maria and Connie were carrying dishes in from the kitchen so Scarlett sat at the table next to Noah. Her Mum would let her know if she needed any more help.

'What are we having?' asked Noah. He was like a little kid at his birthday party. He couldn't hide his excitement, especially from her. He kept looking at her as if he couldn't believe what she'd done. She had been tempted to get one for herself but decided she couldn't justify the expense. And anyway, this was a special gift for Noah.

'You'll see in a minute,' said Esme as she poured wine into everyone's glass except Maria and Noah who had their usual lemon and lime.

'This is all in your honour, bro,' said Joel.

Candy came in carrying a dish of shepherd's pie. 'I was assured this is your favourite meal, Noah, but I added beans and buttered cabbage to make it more interesting. I hope you like it.' Her mum looked so proud of herself and beamed with pleasure.

'I love shepherd's pie, Candy, it's spot on.' Scarlett hoped he was hungry. Candy wouldn't let him up from the table until the shepherd's pie had all gone.

For a while there was no sound but the scraping of knives and forks on plates, and the murmurs of appreciation.

'How do you normally celebrate birthdays in the Whittaker family?' asked Candy.

'We don't,' said Noah. 'We're quite boring compared to the McBride's. We get cards for each other but don't tend to bother with presents.' He shrugged as if it was of no importance.

'How sad,' said Maria.

'We've always made a fuss of birthdays, haven't we Mum?' said Scarlett.

'Oh yes, any excuse for a party and the McBride's are there.'

'I think that's a very healthy attitude, Candy—live life to the full.'

Scarlett suspected that Noah hadn't had many close relationships with his fear of getting it wrong. Something bad must have happened to him to put up such a strong shield against other people. She loved the fact that he got on well with her Mum. They seemed at ease with each other. Most people loved Candy as she was so outgoing and friendly.

What would it be like tomorrow at Latin Nights? She wished it was just the two families, but Miranda would be there and other people from the hospital. She didn't think Noah would enjoy being the centre of attention but he would put up with it for the sake of everyone else. Scarlett had been practising the salsa with Esme and on her own watching YouTube videos. She couldn't wait to show off her newly acquired skills.

Noah couldn't remember the last time he'd been excited at the thought of his birthday. He wasn't sure he ever had, but this year was different. He'd already spent a pleasant evening with the McBrides. He had received an amazing birthday cake, and gifts, the highlight of which had been the one from Scarlett.

She'd bought him the perfect present. Ever since he was a teenager, his dream had been to race a Lamborghini around a race track and Scarlett had made his wish come true. The only other person who knew about the dream was Joel, who had assured him he hadn't told Scarlett. She'd worked it out for herself. Clever girl.

And now it was Saturday night.

He'd chosen his clothes with more care than usual for his Salsa Extravaganza at Latin Nights. Normally he would have worn jeans, a T-shirt and trainers. This time he wore suit trousers and a matching waistcoat over a white shirt. He wore the shirt open necked and rolled the sleeves up to his elbows. Smart black shoes that he'd polished to a shine he could see his face in. He couldn't decide whether he was on trend or it made him look old. He had noticed a man wearing a similar outfit at one of the salsa classes so decided to try it himself.

He arrived with Esme and Joel to find the place packed. There were three times the number of people who turned up for the Friday lessons. The salsa extravaganzas were obviously popular.

The rest of the McBrides were already there and Candy and Connie were strutting their stuff on the dance floor.

Soon after some of the staff from the unit arrived including Miranda and Ashley, a young male social worker.

'Happy birthday, Noah,' said Miranda kissing him on the cheek.

'Yeah, happy birthday,' said Ashley with a big grin.

'Thanks you two, really appreciate it.'

'We're going to dance now,' said Miranda, 'Catch you later. Come on lover.' She grabbed Ashley's hand and pulled him in the direction of the dancers.

Noah watched them as, hand in hand, they found an empty area on the dance floor and moved smoothly into the basics. They soon progressed to more advanced steps with lots of turns and intricate arm movements. It was clear they were experienced dancers. They were so accomplished that their feet seemed to glide over the floor. They made it look effortless.

'Do you think they're an item? They look close.' Scarlett had joined him and he was about to put his arm around her waist and pull her closer to his side when he noticed what she was wearing.

He took her hand and looked her up and down. She wore a short red ballroom dress decorated with sequins and tassels. It clung to her body and accentuated her slim figure. Her hair was loose and swung around her shoulders.

'Like what you see?' she asked with a grin.

'You look lovely.' She looked exquisite and his heart was doing a salsa of its own.

'Thanks. And may I say Dr Whittaker that you look sexy in that waistcoat?'

'Do I? I wasn't sure about it—'

'It's perfect.'

They turned their attention back to Miranda and Ashley.

'My guess is yes, they are together. She called him lover which is a bit of a giveaway. Hasn't she confided in you?' They were living under the same roof.

'She's not said a word. She never tells us anything. They are good, aren't they? Maybe they're here together so they can dance with someone at their level of expertise. It's not much fun dancing with a partner who doesn't know what they're doing.'

'They are good. I don't really know what I'm doing. I only know a few steps.' Even though he'd attended four lessons, he didn't feel at all confident.

'The only difference between them and us is experience. They've been dancing longer than us that's all. And you know the remedy for that, don't you?' She raised her eyebrows questioningly.

'Practice?' His mouth curved into a smile.

'Exactly. Practice, practice and more practice.' She tried to sound like a stern schoolmistress, but her eyes were shooting green sparks and her lips twitched as she tried and failed to hide a smile.

'So we better find a space on that overcrowded dance floor then.'

'Come on, let's dance.'

Scarlett twirled and twisted, and her hair was like a curtain of fire as it flew behind her. When she came back into hold, her body was in exactly the correct position. As he was leading, he decided to mix it up and do a sidestep. She anticipated his move and her hips gyrated in perfect time, the tassels on the dress swaying to the music.

'You've been practising,' he said.

Scarlett threw her head back and laughed. Her slender, white neck was like alabaster—smooth and unlined.

'You noticed! Yay! I have been practising. I want to be good at this. Esme's been helping me.'

Why hadn't Esme said anything to him? He could have joined in.

When they got tired they joined the others at the table.

'Are you having a good time birthday boy?' asked Connie.

'I am, Connie, thank you.'

'Good. I've learned two steps, so… do you wanna dance?

'Of course.' He grinned at Connie. 'Lead the way.'

CHAPTER NINETEEN

Scarlett watched Noah dancing with Connie. Considering she had never done salsa before she was making a good job of the few steps she had learned. Miranda and Ashley were still dancing up a storm, their arms moving almost as much as their legs as they executed advanced routines. They weren't speaking, concentrating on the dance.

What was the deal with those two? She hoped they were an item as then Miranda wouldn't be interested in Noah. She watched them closely for clues as they tore up the dance floor with their stunning displays of athleticism. She tried to follow their movements but their feet moved too fast.

Then Noah came back to the table. Connie was still on the dance floor dancing with a young man.

'Are you enjoying your party?' she asked moving up to let Noah sit next to her. Their arms were touching and she wondered how he would react if she took his hand. She had an overwhelming need to touch him.

'I am, thank you.' He took a sip of his lemonade. Then his phone rang, breaking the mood, and he got up. 'I need to get this. Be back in a sec.' 'Okay.' She watched as he left the club. Strange. Who would be ringing him at this time?

Anton and Esme were dancing together now and Joel was standing at the bar watching them.

Noah came back in with a frown on his handsome face. 'I need to go back to the hospital for a short while. I will return, I promise, but there's an emergency I need to see to first.'

'What emergency? Which patient is it?'

'I'll be back soon.' He hurried out of the club.

Scarlett stared at his receding figure trying to make sense of it. He was off duty which meant that any emergency would be dealt with by the doctor on call. It must be one of his private patients. She sighed and prepared to wait until he returned. She wasn't in the mood for dancing now. The only person she wanted to dance with was Noah.

Noah met Celine at his rooms. She was sitting on the step waiting for him and she was clutching what looked like a bottle of whisky. His heart sank until he walked up to her and realised the bottle hadn't been opened.

'Come in, Celine and make yourself comfy.'

'You look nice. Going somewhere?' she asked. Noah was pleased to see she was sober but looked as if she had been crying.

'I've been with some friends.'

'What's the occasion?'

'It's my birthday.' He'd been enjoying it as well. But Celine needed him and he wasn't going to let her down. She was more important than any birthday celebration.

'Why didn't you tell me on the phone?' Celine asked him angrily. 'I wouldn't have dragged you away from your party. I feel awful now.

Worse than I did when I rang and that was bad enough.' She sat hunched in the chair clutching the whisky bottle.

'Why don't you tell me what's wrong? I said I was here for you whenever you needed me and that means any time of the day or night.' He was determined not to let Celine down. She needed him. This is the reason he became a psychiatrist. To help people like her.

'I bought this bottle on the way home from my agents. There's no work at the moment and I feel useless. I thought that I'd be able to drown my sorrows and feel less useless. But I knew that was wrong. I've been staring at this bottle for an hour. I didn't know what else to do, Noah, I'm sorry. You have a life. A better one than mine and you should be allowed to get on with it.'

'Celine. I am here for you. I'll always be here. You can ring me any time you need help.' He meant it and tried to convince Celine that he was sincere. He would never let her down, not the way he'd let Dom down. She was the important one as were the rest of his patients.

'Where was the party?'

'At a salsa club. It was my sister-in-law's idea. She's very good at salsa.'

'I bet you're good at salsa, Noah. You are the kind of man who's good at anything he turns his hand to. I know you, you're a rock. Reliable. Steadfast. A man among men.'

Noah wanted to tell Celine that she was wrong. He was just like her. Every day was a battle. Every social event a struggle. He wanted to tell her that it got easier as time went on, but it doesn't. You have to be on your guard constantly. If he thought for a moment that it would benefit Celine to hear that he was an alcoholic too, he'd tell her. It wasn't what she needed to hear. She needed a strong person that she could rely on for help. He could be strong for her.

'Celine? Have you contacted any of the AA groups I told you about? I gave you a leaflet, remember? I think you'll find it beneficial to talk about the cravings. They'll be able to help.'

'No, but I will. I just want to give you this. Maybe you could take it to the party.'

He reluctantly took the bottle. 'Thank you. Do you want to talk about anything?'

'No. I've taken up enough of your time. I'm fine now I've spoken to you. Go and enjoy the rest of your birthday and thanks, Noah, for being there for me.'

She seemed calm now and he felt he could leave her safely.

'Will you be alright?'

'Of course I will. I didn't open the bottle. I feel I've made a small step in the right direction.' She smiled and he nodded.

'You've made a massive step. You should be proud. I am.'

Noah hurried back to the club clutching the bottle of whisky. When he walked up to the table, Joel stared in horror at what he was carrying.

'Don't look like that. I've just seen one of my private patients and she gave me this to prevent her opening it herself. Here, you take it.'

'Right. How are you feeling?' Joel looked concerned and he hurried to reassure him.

'I feel good. She didn't open it and neither did I. That's two alcoholics saved from getting drunk tonight.'

'I'm proud of you,' said Joel. He looked emotional. Joel was one of the few people who knew the whole story and he was glad he had his brother's love and support.

'Can I get you a drink?' asked Joel.

'Mineral water please.'

While Joel was at the bar, Noah looked for Scarlett. She was dancing with Anton and looked as if she was enjoying herself immensely.
He loved watching her dance. She had a natural grace and rhythm
as she turned and twirled. He could have watched her all night.

'There you are,' said Candy who sat down next to him. 'We
wondered where you'd gone.'

'A medical emergency. One of my private patients. It's all good
now. Do you want to dance?'

'I'd love to. I thought you'd never ask.'

They got up and joined the dancers. Candy was good at salsa.
Better than him. But somehow they danced well together.

'I must say, Noah, Scarlett said you're a workaholic and she's right.
Fancy having to see a patient on your birthday. Wasn't there anyone
else who could have seen the patient?'

'I'm afraid not. I couldn't let her down.'

'Well, you're a star, being so dedicated. I hope the patients appreciate you.'

'All in a day's work,' he said smiling.

'You're back,' said Scarlett when she spotted him.

They changed over and Noah found himself dancing with Scarlett. Candy was dancing with Anton.

He took Scarlett into hold and realised that it was starting to feel
more natural now. Or was it because it was Scarlett he held in his
arms? They seemed to fit together perfectly when they were dancing, moving together as one. Would they fit together in other, more
intimate, ways? He couldn't let his mind go there, but sometimes
his mind got the upper hand and the images of the two of them
together wouldn't leave him.

'Your Mum's a good dancer,' Noah said, trying to distract his
errant thoughts.

'She is. She used to do it seriously before having us lot. I think she
could have been a professional.'

'I think you're right.'

'So, is Celine okay now?'

'How did you know it was Celine?'

'Educated guess.' Scarlett was gazing at him with a questioning look.

'She is. I did tell her to ring me whenever she needed to.'

'Why did you give her your mobile number?' Scarlett wasn't smiling now. In fact she looked annoyed.

'She's one of my private patients now. She's struggling and I know what that's like. I need to be there for her.'

'You can't be on call twenty-four seven, Noah.' Scarlett frowned. He knew she was thinking of him, but she didn't understand how driven he felt to help people like Celine.

'I can if that's what it takes.'

Scarlett didn't want to argue with Noah. It was important for busy medical staff to have their down time, but Noah was a law unto himself as the saying went and she wasn't prepared to ruin a lovely evening by arguing. She had waited impatiently for him to return so she could dance with him again. The last thing she wanted was to annoy him.

She smiled, hoping to regain the good mood of before. It was his birthday after all and they were celebrating. She wanted to regain the feeling of fun and the closeness they had achieved. There wasn't much time. Scarlett was aware that the evening was drawing to a close. A lot of people had already left, and there were fewer couples on the dance floor.

'We're going now,' said her mum. 'Maria is staying at home tonight. You can too if you want.' She smiled at Scarlett and then at Noah. They had stopped dancing to say goodbye.

'Thanks, but it's okay. I'll see you soon.'

'Okay then. Thanks for a great party, Noah and enjoy the rest of it,' Candy said.

Esme and Joel were the next ones to leave. Scarlett looked around to see if any of their group were still in the club. Everyone had gone, even Miranda and Ashley.

'Just us,' she said to Noah. It reminded her of the wedding reception when she'd more or less begged him to spend the night with her.

'Yes. Do you want another drink?'

'No thanks.'

'Do you want to keep dancing?'

'Maybe one last dance before they close the club.'

Once again he took her into hold and she felt her spirits soar. This was what she was meant for she decided as she twirled, moved her hips in the sensual flow of the salsa. Problem was, she didn't feel this way with any other man. Only Noah made her feel as if they could fly.

Every time his gaze met hers, her heart turned over and her pulse pounded.

The end of the evening arrived too quickly. The music stopped and everyone except Noah and Scarlett left the dance floor.

'So…' she said.

'So,' he replied.

They stared into each other's eyes and Scarlett realised that this was it. Crunch time. Her body ached for his touch and she fought an inner battle. Should they just go home separately having had a wonderful evening? Or… did she risk rejection again?

'I want to spend the night with you. I promise I won't regret it in the morning, I'm not drunk and I don't expect anything to come from this. Just one night, that's all I'm asking.'

'Are you absolutely sure?' His voice was husky and her skin tingled.

Noah studied her face, so she raised her eyebrows in a—hopefully—appealing way. She couldn't read his expression, he remained a closed book.

'I've never been surer.' As she said the words she realised how true they were. She wanted him. She wasn't going to think any further than this night. It would be a lovely memory for her to revisit on days when she was struggling. She didn't even care if the sex wasn't all that good. It might not be the first time. First and last time, she had to keep that in mind.

Then all rational thought fled as he took her in his arms and kissed her. The gentleness surprised her, but the kiss promised more... much more and a shiver ran through her body at the thought.

CHAPTER TWENTY

Noah woke first and lay on his side watching Scarlett sleep. Last night had been amazing. A perfect ending to the evening. He'd been a bit surprised, but pleased, that Scarlett had suggested they spend the night together. This time he couldn't say no. She only wanted one night. No commitment. No strings. So one night was all they would have.

And what a night. Neither of them had held back. The longing and anticipation had given them a sense of urgency and they'd responded to each other with overwhelming need. They stoked the gently growing fire so it became a flame that threatened to consume them both.

Just thinking of it made Noah's need for Scarlett grow and he was on the point of waking her up when she opened her eyes.

'Good morning to you.'

'Good morning to you too.' Scarlett's hair was spread over the pillow and her green eyes were half closed. She obviously took a while to wake up.

She reached for him and he stroked her hair back from her face. He didn't want to leave her but they had agreed on one night and that night was over. He should go.

Then she kissed him and he responded. Their lovemaking was slow and sweet, unlike the more urgent coupling of the night before. He wanted it to go on forever, but eventually it was over and time for them to get back to normal. He could only imagine how difficult that was going to be.

'I need to go,' he whispered.

'Do you have to?' she asked sleepily.

'Yes. Last night was… well, beyond my wildest dreams, but…'

'But that was then, this is now?' she asked sadly.

'Something like that.'

He thought briefly of staying. Spending the day with Scarlett. Having a nice relaxing Sunday. Maybe go for a walk in the park. Then go back to bed… Scarlett was watching him and he needed to be the strong one. He kissed her gently, trying not to notice the look of reproach in her eyes. She had said one night only.

When Noah eventually left the house he headed straight for the gym.

Noah pounded the treadmill. He had a surplus of nervous energy and didn't know how to get rid of it. The gym was quiet for a Sunday and he was thankful for that. He needed to think and didn't want to talk to anyone else.

Last night had been a revelation. He knew sex with Scarlett would be good. He didn't know how he knew, he just did. But he had no idea it would affect him as much as it had.

Scarlett was beautiful and she had given herself to him so willingly, joyfully, that the sex had been amazing. She was amazing and his feelings for her were deepening. He still needed to protect her from himself and keep his distance, but it would be so hard, if not impossible, when every instinct he possessed wanted her.

He'd fought to repress this feeling but the time he had spent with Scarlett had stopped that in its tracks and opened his heart to emotions he shouldn't have. He had no choice now, he would have to be strong and resist her. He should never have agreed to spend the night with her, but she had caught him when he was feeling mellow, having had a great birthday, been spoiled rotten by the McBride's and had the most beautiful woman he had ever met in his arms. Nothing had changed. He couldn't risk falling for her as he would only let her down. It couldn't happen again.

He showered quickly and drove home.

The house was silent. Too silent. Scarlett wondered whether she should go to Mum's or maybe Esme's. But no, Noah would be there and he might think she wanted more than they'd agreed. He'd be right. She mustn't let him think she was stalking him.

It was a beautiful summer day, with deep blue skies and little fluffy clouds. She should be out enjoying it.

A short time later, she was in the garden, looking for things that needed doing. Weeding always needed doing, so she fetched the tools from the shed and set to. She wore a hat and long sleeves. With her fair skin she couldn't risk getting sunburnt.

Scarlett couldn't stop thinking about Noah. They got on well together, both at work and socially. She felt comfortable in his presence, until he touched her, or looked at her in a certain way, then he could have suggested flying to the moon and she would have gone with him.

And the sex… she'd never known it could be like that. It made all her previous experiences with men pale into insignificance. She had never been as turned on as she'd been with Noah. Just the thought of his mouth on her skin made her temperature rise and her heart beat wildly.

What did it all mean? Was she in love, or was it pure lust? Never having been in love before she wasn't sure, but why did it have to be him? He'd made his feelings known. He didn't want commitment, marriage or any of that. So, whatever it was, there was no future for them. But the thought of what they'd shared the previous night would be etched forever on her brain. She wanted more, but how much more she wasn't really sure. Nothing had changed though, had it? They were still work colleagues related by marriage. Perhaps that was all they'd ever be.

Scarlett dragged a weed out of the soil and put it in the basket. Poor weed, it wasn't wanted. She felt sorry for that weed. Growing happily in its own little bit of the garden, minding its own business, then—wham! Dragged out by its roots and abandoned. Destined for the compost heap.

Scarlett took a deep drink from her water bottle. The sun was quite hot and she'd probably have to abandon the gardening soon. Come back later in the afternoon when the air was cooler.

How should she act tomorrow when she saw Noah? Pretend it hadn't happened? She couldn't do that and she hoped he wouldn't either. It had been a great night and she didn't regret a thing. If that was all she'd ever have of him, at least she had the memory of their first and last night together.

How could she have thought that one night would be enough? Now she knew how good they were together, she wanted more. Should she suggest to Noah that they do it again? What if he said no? Maybe last night was all he'd wanted and now he could get on with his life and forget about her. She couldn't face that kind of rejection. How humiliating it would be. No, she couldn't tell him how she felt. It was better to leave things as they were.

The following Monday, Scarlett got a text from her mum asking her to join them for a family meal that evening. When Candy summoned her girls, they never refused. It was tradition. It meant she had something of highest importance to tell them.

Scarlett was not in the mood for a family meal. Lovely as it was to be together with her mum and sisters, there was always an ulterior motive. Before Esme got together with Joel she was the subject of Mum's worry and concern, and rightly so, Esme had been in a dark place, living a half-life. But now she was radiant. Joel's love for her had restored the real Esme.

The position of sister-who-needed-help had now passed to Scarlett. She was the next to get married, as tradition dictated. Her Mum would want to be kept up-to-date with developments. There hadn't been any. She and Noah had spent the night together but the agreement was only one night, so that was the end of that. And she wasn't going to tell her family about their one night stand.

Scarlett was waiting for the questions to start, but they ate their lasagne and salad—with a vegetable one for Maria—drank home-made lemonade as a change from wine with Esme extolling the virtues of married life and no mention of boyfriends at all.

'I expect you'll be wondering why I got you all here today? It's to talk about the shop launching the sale of teas and coffees. Dot and I have decided that the first of August would be a good time to start. We need to advertise the event and think of a way to bring in custom. We could give free drinks up until midday, for instance.'

'How are you going to advertise it?' asked Esme.

'Well I thought of flyers to give out to customers and even post them through people's letterboxes. We want it to be a grand opening.

We've got plenty of time between now and the first of August, as it's only June.'

'What about a website?' asked Connie.

'If we had someone who was good at IT that would be a possibility.'

'I'll do it,' said Connie.

'Thank you, darling. Yes, you would be the best candidate for the job, given you're the youngest and will be *au fait* with modern technology.'

Scarlett listened to the family throwing ideas into the pot and tried to think of something to add. But her mind wasn't on coffee and websites, she couldn't stop thinking about Noah. They had been civil to each other when they met for work that morning. All the lovely warm closeness had vanished like mist in the sun. She hadn't expected him to be all lovey-dovey at work, of course she hadn't. But he could have given her a sign, some acknowledgement that they'd spent the night together.

'And you could offer an alternative to dairy, like oat milk, or coconut milk for the vegans,' said Maria. 'In fact, you should probably offer vegan cakes as well.'

'And gluten free,' said Esme. 'That's a very good idea, Maria.'

'Will do,' said Connie, 'And I'll think up some ideas for the website. Lots of bright colours and pictures of the cakes.'

'I'll help,' said Maria.

Candy clapped her hands. 'I knew my lovely girls would be brimming with ideas. Thank you, darlings, I'm so glad you're all on board with this. Put the date in your diaries, I really need all of you there. Now, what's your news? I'm all ears. Scarlett? Anything to report?' She knew it. This was the real reason her mum had got them together.

'About what Mum?' Play the innocent and stall for time.

'Well… anything. How are you getting on with Noah? Everything alright between you?'

'Fine. Why wouldn't it be?' Talk about cutting to the chase.

'He was seen,' said Connie accusingly but with a grin on her face.

'I beg your pardon?' Plead ignorance until she explained herself, although Scarlett had no idea what was coming.

'Pizza First. My advice, dear sister, is that if Noah wants to keep his liaisons secret, he shouldn't sit on the table in the window. Matt saw him when he was in town,' Connie said.

'Who with?' Scarlett tried for nonchalant, as if she didn't care who Noah went out with. She knew the answer before Connie spoke.

'Miranda.'

CHAPTER TWENTY-ONE

It was a warm July evening, three days before the open day at Candy Dots cake shop. The days were still long, and the skies still light until about nine, and Scarlett and Esme were efficiently and methodically distributing flyers in the nearby houses. Maria and Connie had worked hard together at producing a bright, colourful document that looked good as a large poster to be put in the window and on the wall inside the shop. It also functioned as a flyer to be posted through private letterboxes and given out to the shops and offices in the immediate area around Leytonsfield town centre.

After about an hour they stopped for a rest on a bench outside the post office. Why the bench was there nobody really knew, but it was useful for elderly people resting their weary bones and sisters delivering flyers.

'There are some lovely gardens. You have to get off the main roads to appreciate how much care people take of their homes. We're very lucky to live in Leytonsfield, don't you think?'

'I do, Esme,' said Scarlett. 'Do you think you and Joel will always live here?'

'I hope so. I don't think he's got any desire to go back to Manchester.'

'Good. I hope you stay here too. Great place to bring up kids.' Scarlett cast a sidelong glance at Esme. She remembered what their mum had said about there being a baby announcement by the end of the year. Scarlett was coming around to the idea of being an aunty.

'Can I talk to you about something?' asked Scarlett. She had to confide in someone soon or she'd burst. She wasn't the kind of person who kept everything locked away deep inside her and who better to talk to and seek advice from than her older sister?

'Of course, Scarlett, you know that. You can talk to me about anything.' Esme sat sideways on the bench so she could face her.

'After the salsa extravaganza, Noah and I spent the night together.'

'I see. I noticed that you were spending a lot of time with him, especially on the dance floor, and then when Noah didn't come home… That's good news, Scarlett, I'm pleased. Everyone likes Noah.' She smiled but Scarlett couldn't return it.

'It was a one-off. There'll be no repeat.' Saying it out loud made it seem so final.

'Has Noah told you that himself?' Esme looked worried now, but there was more to tell her.

'Not in so many words, no, but the following Monday at work, he carried on as if nothing had happened. He was friendly, but no more than he was with anyone else.' She remembered meeting him in the corridor and he said good morning then kept on walking. It was almost as if the weekend hadn't happened. It took all her strength and will power not to burst into tears. She hadn't expected him to be all over her like a rash—she wasn't sure what she'd expected really—but to be treated as if she was just another member of staff after what they'd shared the night before was too much.

Scarlett had sworn to herself that she would behave the same way. A polite smile was all he was receiving from her from now on. And only then if she was in the mood. How dare he blank her like that? He had been friendlier with Miranda at the team meeting. Scarlett hardly spoke a word. Noah didn't seem to notice or care.

And then there was the night Matt had seen Noah and Miranda together in Pizza First. She had fully intended to ask Miranda about it but had chickened out. At least she'd paid them the rent and the advance, so both herself and Maria were back in the black.

There was something else that she'd been trying very hard not to think about. She'd missed a period. She'd been feeling tired and had gone right off coffee. All symptoms of pregnancy. She knew the only sensible thing to do was to buy a pregnancy test kit, but she kept hoping her period would start and that would be that.

'You know you should talk to him. It's the only way you'll find out what's really going on. The biggest mistake I made when I began to have feelings for Joel was to keep it all to myself. If I'd just spoken to him, it would have saved us a lot of heartache and misunderstandings. I'm sure it's the same in your situation.' Esme took a swig from her water bottle. It was warm with the sun on them, despite the lateness of the day.

'I appreciate what you're saying, Esme, and I wish it was as simple as that. You see, I asked Noah to spend the night with me. I told him I didn't want anything else from him, just that one night and he's taken me at my word. I know he doesn't want commitment, so there's no point talking to him.'

'I disagree. There's always a point in talking, even if it's to confirm what you think you already know. His feelings could have changed too.' Esme watched her and Scarlett wished she could be more like her sister. She was still tanned from her honeymoon and looked even more beautiful than ever.

But is what she was advising the best way to go? It would be lovely to find that Noah wanted her after all. Not just for one night, but permanently. She was feeling particularly vulnerable, not knowing if she was pregnant or not. She could be worrying for nothing. She'll get her period in a day or so, she was sure. She knew she should do the test and not wait for something that may not happen, but she was scared. What if she was pregnant? What then?

Why did love have to be so complicated?

'I owe you an apology,' Noah said the next day as he posted a flyer through the letterbox of the last in a row of cottages. Scarlett was waiting by the gate.

'Why is that?' They hadn't had the chance to talk as Noah had delivered his flyers at the speed of light, leaving Scarlett behind. He'd been quiet, obviously not wanting to talk to her, so she'd lagged behind, trying to stay away from him. Nothing had changed at work, he was still polite and keeping his distance. She was doing the same.

'How about we go for a drink and I'll tell you all about it?'

'Okay. Let's go to the Bull's Head and we can sit in the beer garden. If you're okay with going to a pub?' She couldn't imagine what he had to apologise for but was eager to hear it.

'Yes, it's fine. Good idea.'

They set off, Scarlett keeping her distance from Noah. Should she link him? Or would that seem too proprietary? Just being with him set her nerves tingling. He walked with long, purposeful strides and she hurried to keep up with him.

It was a gorgeous, hot summer evening and Candy Dots open day was only two days away. All the flyers had been posted and the website was up and running, and already getting hundreds of hits.

Life would be perfect if it wasn't for one small thing. Scarlett was aching to tell Noah how she felt about him. She was in love, she knew that now. Her mind was spinning with what-ifs. What if she was pregnant? What if she told him her fears?

Her period hadn't arrived. She might be pregnant and she had no idea how Noah would react if she was. He wouldn't be pleased, of that she was sure. Would he stand by her though? It could bring them closer. Or it could drive them further apart. And what did she really feel about being a mother? It shouldn't be happening, that was all she could focus on.

They got their drinks and settled in the beer garden. There were a few families there with young children. Little ones chased each other around the tables. The sound of their laughter carried over to where Scarlett and Noah were sitting. One family had a very young baby, only a few weeks old Scarlett would have guessed. A little girl dressed all in pink and wrapped in a lacy white shawl. She was absolutely gorgeous and Scarlett couldn't take her eyes off her.

Scarlett looked at Noah to see if he had noticed her staring at the baby and was about to make some comment or other. He himself was staring at the infant with a smile on his lips and an affectionate look. Maybe he was thinking of himself as an uncle. Just because someone admired a tiny baby didn't mean they wanted one themselves.

'So, what's this apology then?' Scarlett spoke more sharply than she intended but it did the trick and got Noah's attention back on her.

'I haven't behaved very well towards you the last few weeks, and I apologise for that.'

'In what way?' She knew the answer, but she wanted to hear him articulate it.

'The night we spent together was amazing. Instead of getting it out of my system, as I thought it would do, it's made me want you more. But that can't happen, so I put up barriers which I realise now could have been hurtful. I never want to hurt you, Scarlett, you must believe that. I can't risk getting involved with someone, but I just wanted you to know that I deeply regret upsetting you and trying to push you away.' He sat, his head down, his fingers loosely linked and stared at the ground.

'Why can't you risk getting involved with someone? Is it something to do with your student days? Did someone hurt you?' Noah had opened up and Scarlett was determined to take advantage of that and get to the bottom of why he didn't want a relationship.

'Yes, it was in my student days, but I hurt them, not the other way around. I let them down.'

'Do you want to talk about it?' She sensed she was getting closer to the real Noah. If only he would tell her what happened, maybe she could help.

'Not right now. I will tell you, soon, but it doesn't change anything. I hope we can still be friends. You're a very special person, Scarlett, and I wish things could be different.'

'I understand.' Why did she say that? She didn't understand, not really. What was this thing that was keeping them apart? Something from his past. Something that was stopping him falling in love and letting a woman get close to him. She needed to know what it was. Without understanding why he was so cautious, they could never move forward. And she wanted to move forward with Noah, more than she'd ever wanted anything else.

'You're quiet, Scarlett. What are you thinking?'

Noah had hated himself for treating Scarlett so shabbily, even though he had no choice. He was doing it for her own good but wasn't able to explain why. She deserved better than him. She should be showered with love, gifts and happy times. He was too messed up to risk her depending on him in any way. He'd let her down and if that happened he couldn't live with himself.

He was growing too fond of the bubbly redhead who kept him on his toes. She had become part of his life, despite trying to keep her at a distance.

'Just about the open day tomorrow. I hope it goes well for Mum and Dot. They've put so much effort and love into their business. We need to help them all we can. You'll be there, won't you?'

'Of course. I'll be glad to play a part.'

Scarlett's phone rang and she pulled it out of her pocket and smiled when she saw who it was. 'Hi Sadie, nice to hear from you.'

Sadie. One of her friends from uni. She sounded happy now, back to her normal self.

'Good news?'

'Yes. Sadie's coming to stay for a few days. She wants to be here for the open day. She's a good friend.'

'When is she coming?'

'Tomorrow. She's willing to help in any way she can, so we'll have another pair of hands. It'll be lovely to have her all to myself even for a short time. Normally Megs is with her but she's got a new boyfriend and the men always come first with her.'

'Sisters before misters.'

Scarlett laughed. 'That's it.'

'Are we good?' he asked quietly. 'I hope we can still be friends. You're very special to me you know.' He really wished things could be different. But they were bound to meet up in family events as well as at work. He needed for them to be okay.

After a long silence, Scarlett nodded. 'Yes, we're okay.'

CHAPTER TWENTY-TWO

The first day of August dawned bright and clear. Perfect weather for the open day.

Six of them would get to the shop early to start breakfast and drinks. Scarlett was in the first group with Candy, Dot, Dot's daughter Bernice, Esme and Sadie.

When Scarlett and Sadie arrived at Candy Dots, the others were already there.

'Oh my goodness, Scarlett… what are you wearing?' cried Dot.

Scarlett did a twirl. 'Do you like it? It's a cupcake girl costume. Connie is wearing one too. I didn't think the rest of you would be brave enough to join us, so I've got you something else to wear instead.'

Scarlett's dress had short puff sleeves, a bodice with a huge pink bow and a short skirt in pink satin with cupcakes embroidered all around it. She wore a pink wig with a cake hat attached, pink stockings with blue bows at the top and silver shoes with a good sized heel.

'You'll be sorry you wore those heels at the end of the day,' said Dot, 'Your feet will be barking like Crazy Boy.'

'Don't worry, I'll take them off.' Scarlett was reminded of the last time she took her shoes off when Noah carried her home. She pushed the thought from her mind. Today was for fun and helping Dot and Candy make a success of the business. Channelling her inner Scarlett O'Hara, she'd think about the rest of it tomorrow.

'What have you got for us to wear, darling?' said Candy.

'Aprons with the shop's name on them and crocheted cupcake hats. They are optional as they could be too hot in this weather.'

'Oh lovely! Let's have a look.'

When they were all dressed in their aprons and hats, they took selfies and a selection of group photos for the website.

'We want everyone to take away the message that we know how to have fun,' said Scarlett.

The shop had never looked so good, inside and out. Sylvia from the Little Flower Shop had donated two hanging baskets and two tubs of flowers in assorted colours. From the little she'd learned from Esme about plants, the baskets contained fuchsias with pink and purple flowers, and the tubs were full of brightly coloured petunias.

Bunting adorned the walls inside and large posters designed by Connie and Maria listed all the drinks now available.

Candy decided that Scarlett should be front of house, so she served the customers while Sadie and Bernice cooked breakfasts.

'How are you feeling?' Sadie asked quietly before going into the kitchen to help Bernice.

Scarlett had told her friend everything that was happening with Noah. Sadie was the most grounded and sensible person she knew and always gave good advice. She had agreed with Esme that Scarlett needed to talk to Noah. She had also told her that she thought she might be pregnant. Sadie advised caution, it could simply be stress brought on by everything that had happened lately.

'I haven't come on yet but feel bloated and pre-menstrual.' Scarlett always had symptoms a week before her periods.

'Well, there you are then,' said Sadie, 'That could be the answer. Although it wouldn't hurt to do a test just in case.'

At nine o'clock Scarlett heard Joel and Noah arrive.

'Hi, welcome and thanks for offering to help,' said Candy.

'No problem. How are sales?' Joel asked.

'Slowly picking up. We're mainly being asked for lattes and cappuccinos.'

Scarlett stepped out of the kitchen and into the front of the shop.

'Wow! You look amazing,' said Joel. Noah smiled but said nothing. As usual he was keeping his thoughts to himself.

'Right,' said Candy clapping her hands like an infant teacher, 'Shall we do some swapsies? Scarlett and Noah can do drinks, Esme and Joel in the kitchen and I'll serve with Sadie.'

Scarlett glanced at Noah. She hoped they could be friendly today. He had apologised for the way he'd treated her, so she was determined to be forgiving. 'What d'you think? Fancy yourself as a barista?'

'I'll try anything once,' said Noah. He was wearing a pale blue polo shirt and blue denim jeans. It would make a good uniform as he looked quite the professional. Another idea for the suggestions box. She handed him an apron to wear.

'What shall I do?' asked Dot.

'You have a sit down, Mum, and rest that hip,' said Bernice. Poor Dot was on the waiting list for a hip replacement and suffered in silence a lot of the time. Dot took a chair outside and sat just to the left of the open door so she could hand out flyers to passers-by.

'Two cappuccinos, a latte and one English Breakfast tea,' called Candy.

'Right, that's us,' said Scarlett grinning.

Noah watched carefully as Scarlett showed him how to use Puffing Billy as Candy had named the coffee machine. He got the coffee cups and lids ready and Scarlett did the rest.

Noah was standing close to her watching eagerly. He frowned slightly as she demonstrated how to make the perfect cappuccino, then smiled when she made a pattern on the foam on the top.

'It's not perfect but it can take years of practice to get it exactly right.'

'Looks good to me,' said Noah, which gave her the warm fuzzies.

After a short while Noah was allowed to have a go at making the coffees. He took his time, following Scarlett's instructions meticulously.

'I never realised there was so much to learn about making a cup of coffee.'

'We're professionals, we like to get it right,' said Scarlett, 'But well done, not bad for your first attempt.' She hoped she didn't sound too patronising.

Maria and Connie arrived at eleven o'clock with more cakes, biscuits and buns. Connie looked sweet in her cupcake dress and more selfies were taken.

By late afternoon, the stream of customers had decreased to a trickle. The long day was drawing to a close.

'I think it's time to wrap it up for today,' said Candy, 'Thank you everyone for your help, it's been wonderful how you've all rallied round to make our open day so successful. Of course we won't know precisely how much extra we've earned until we count the takings.'

'Yes, thanks from me too,' Dot said, 'We couldn't have done it without you.'

As people moved to clean the machines and generally tidy up the shop, Joel and Esme stood together with their arms around each other. Esme was blushing and Joel cleared his throat.

'W-we have an announcement to make before you all shoot off.'

Scarlett didn't need to be told the nature of the announcement, it was written all over their faces. She glanced at Noah who smiled and winked.

'I knew it,' said Connie in a stage whisper.

'Shush everyone, let Joel speak,' Candy said almost bursting with excitement.

'Some of you have obviously guessed, but we are pregnant,' said Joel.

'Yay!' shouted Connie, 'We're going to be aunties,' she grabbed Maria and spun her around laughing.

'Congratulations!' shouted Dot, Bernice and Sadie.

'Let me hug you!' Candy threw her arms around Esme and Joel, then Maria and Connie joined in the hug.

Sadie looked at Scarlett who was trying to hold back her tears. 'A baby, how lovely.' Are you okay, Scarlett?'

'Yes. I'm delighted for them…' She brushed angrily at a stray tear that had escaped despite her best efforts to hold them in.

'Here's your share of the leftovers, Sadie.' Candy had bagged up the food that was left and given it out to everyone. Sadie had to return to Manchester so they all hugged her and told her she was a diamond to have worked so hard. She promised to pay another visit shortly.

'Let's not leave it so long next time,' Sadie said.

'I promise. It's been great having you here. Give my love to Megs when you see her,' said Scarlett. She hugged her friend tightly.

'You need to do that test,' whispered Sadie.

'I know,' said Scarlett before letting her go.

Joel and Esme were going back to Candy's, no doubt to continue the celebration of the wonderful baby news. Maria was staying overnight there as well.

'I'll see you home,' Noah said quietly.

'Okay.' She didn't need seeing home as her car was outside, but Scarlett wasn't going to turn down the chance of having Noah to herself for a short while, so didn't mention the car.

CHAPTER
TWENTY-THREE

They'd eaten their share of the food that was left over from the open day and were relaxing in the garden with glasses of lemonade.

Noah was grateful that Miranda had gone out. He'd been contemplating telling Scarlett the truth. He owed it to her to be honest. If he'd thought they could have one night together and then walk away without anything changing, he'd been deluded.

They'd shared a wonderful experience and it had changed everything. He didn't know for sure what Scarlett was thinking and feeling and he daren't ask her. He didn't want to let her down, but he needed to be honest about why he couldn't get involved.

Scarlett had stipulated one night only, so perhaps she didn't want a repeat. Even if they simply stayed friends, they saw each other a lot. Not just at work anymore but socially. Like today which he'd enjoyed immensely. Some women could have looked ridiculous in the outfit Scarlett had worn. She just looked gorgeous, sweet and sexy. She'd changed when she got home to jeans and a T-shirt but still looked good to him.

The late afternoon sun bathed the garden in a soft light. Bees and other insects buzzed peacefully amongst the flowers and Noah let the quiet and tranquillity seep into his soul. Hopefully it would give him the strength to go back in time to his student days which were some of the best and the worst years of his life.

He looked at Scarlett who was watching him. Waiting.

'So, you want to know my secret?' he smiled and she nodded.

'But only if you want to tell me. I'm not going to pressure you.'

'Okay. Well… I found being a medical student difficult. We all did, but some coped better than others. We drank, went on binges, took drugs, anything to get us through it. There were some days when I was so tired I felt ill. We never had time for meal breaks. We barely had time to drink water. It was a wonder we didn't all have kidney failure.' He glanced at Scarlett to see how she was reacting. She was listening closely with an unreadable expression. Not giving anything away. He continued.

'I'd always wanted to be a doctor like my dad. Giving up was not an option. The times I thought about leaving medicine, I pictured my father's look of contempt when I told him. We were a family of doctors and giving up medicine was unthinkable. It worked for me, driving me on when I was at my lowest.'

Noah took a sip of his lemonade. He'd arrived at the point of his story. Could he go on? Tell Scarlett the rest and risk her scorn?

'What happened, Noah?' she asked softly.

'I had a friend called Dom. We shared digs with another medical student. Dom told me he was thinking of leaving medicine as he didn't want to be a doctor anymore. He said he couldn't cope with it any longer; the long hours, the fear of getting something wrong and causing harm. He said he didn't think he was cut out for it and just wanted to go home. His family home was in Wales. He'd found

London a bit of a culture shock.' He stopped, picturing his young friend, his pale face and shy smile.

'Anyway, I gave him the wrong advice. I told him he'd feel better about it eventually. It was hard but it would get easier. I'm not sure I even believed that. He came to me for help and I let him down. I told him what I would have needed to hear should I have been in his situation. To imagine how disappointed his parents would be when he told them. They'd been so proud of him, the first person in their family to become a doctor. He'd been so full of optimism at the start of our training. He felt so lucky to be given the chance.

'I'll never forget the look on his face when I told him not to give up. It was as if he could see the way out of his prison and I slammed the door shut. He looked frightened, trapped.

'A few days later I came back from an horrendous night duty. I'd been on call and spent the whole night running from one emergency to another. One patient died. When I got back to our flat I found Dom. He'd taken his own life.' Scarlett gasped. She had tears running down her cheeks.

Noah put his head in his hands. 'I tried to resuscitate him even though I knew it was hopeless. The paramedics had to drag me off him. He'd gone.'

Noah cried then. Tears for his young friend who'd had his whole life ahead of him. For his parents who should never have had to bury their son. He cried for himself, a naïve, wet behind the ears medical student who knew nothing about life or people and didn't have the sense or maturity to advise anyone about anything.

Scarlett sat next to him with her arm around his shoulders until his tears dried.

'Dom's parents weren't like mine. They just wanted their son to be happy. They would never have condemned him. I shouldn't have tried to advise him, I was entirely the wrong person. I should have kept quiet, pointed him in the direction of a counsellor. Told him to make his own mind up. It was his life. I am the reason he took his life. Me. Nobody else.'

'I think you're being too hard on yourself,' Scarlett said softly.

'I've lived with this for a long time, Scarlett, and I've thought about it over and over. It's haunted my dreams.' A cold despair gripped him. He'd lived with this for so long. He just wanted to be free of it.

He stood up suddenly, not able to sit still. He walked slowly around the garden with Scarlett by his side.

'Have you ever spoken to anyone about it?'

'Yes. I was on the verge of becoming an alcoholic. A high-functioning alcoholic. I did my job and spent the hours in between drunk. I lost a weekend once. Spent the whole time totally off my head. Don't remember a thing. It was time to do something about it, so I started counselling. I haven't touched alcohol for fifteen years and will never drink again.'

'Do your parents know? About Dom I mean?'

'No. My mother thinks I struggled but she doesn't know the extent of it. I'll never tell them. They wouldn't understand.' He shook his head sadly.

'Thank you for telling me. It can't have been easy.'

'But now, Scarlett, you understand why I can't get so close to someone else. I can't risk letting anyone else down again.'

They'd arrived back at the garden bench and sat down. Scarlett put her arm across his shoulders and he breathed in her aroma of coconut shampoo and vanilla. He felt relieved that he'd managed to tell her and she hadn't recoiled in horror. Not that she would have done. As a psychiatric nurse, she'd heard it all before.

'Can I ask you a question?'

'Of course. Ask anything you like.' The hard part was over. He could cope with whatever she wanted to know.

'Since that time, have you ever let anyone else down?'

'No, because I haven't let anyone get close enough. It's why I keep my distance, Scarlett.' She looked thoughtful and Noah waited to hear what she had to say.

'Okay. But what about the people who are close to you? Joel, Esme, your parents?'

'I don't let them rely on me for anything.' He squirmed slightly, imagining letting down the people he loved.

'Not even Joel, your baby brother? He's always looked up to you, that's what Esme says. You've never let him down. And then the patients. They rely on you to help them turn their lives around and you've never let them down. That's why you gave Celine your mobile number isn't it? Because you're scared of letting her down?'

He nodded. 'I told her I'd be on the end of a phone whenever she needs me and I will.'

'What happened to Dom was a tragedy, but it was a one-off.' Scarlett took his hand in hers and he didn't pull away. He relished the physical contact. 'A mistake made by an exhausted, young medical student. You're not that person any more. You're a strong, knowledgeable, consultant psychiatrist. People come to you because of your expertise and you've never let them down and you never will. They all have faith in you for good reason. In fact, the only person who doesn't have faith in you is you.'

Scarlett kept hold of Noah's hand. He needed comfort and who better to provide it than the woman who loved him? She hadn't known what to expect when he began talking. She imagined it might be about a woman, someone he'd been in love with and had let him down, or vice versa. She never thought it would be something as heart-breaking as losing a friend to suicide and then blaming himself. He lived for fifteen years thinking he'd caused his friend's death.

It was a similar story to the one Esme had told. She had suffered a panic attack in the car that her fiancé was driving and the car crashed killing him outright. She had spent the next ten years blaming herself and it wasn't until she had met Joel that her life changed for the better.

Joel had been Esme's saviour. Maybe she could be the same for Noah.

'Thank you for telling me that, Noah, it does explain a lot, but I think it's time you accepted that you're not going to let anyone down, and start letting people in.'

'Thanks for listening. It has helped. You're a good listener.' Noah sounded sad. It had obviously taken it out of him, telling her about Dom. 'But I'm still an alcoholic, and that's not something I want everyone to know. I've got it under control but I'm aware of how easy it would be to fall off the waggon. I'm not a good risk. You deserve better.' His eyes had a haunted look as he gazed at her. She wanted to comfort him, take away the pain, but she wasn't sure how.

'I wish you wouldn't put yourself down like that.'

Scarlett couldn't be too cross with him after he'd opened his heart to her. He'd done a brave thing and should be proud of being so honest. She imagined he was feeling the opposite of proud having just relived one of the worst times of his life.

'I suppose I should go,' he said reluctantly.

'You don't have to,' she replied.

Noah didn't answer and Scarlett guessed he was still wrestling his demons.

'We don't have to do anything. Just be together. It might help.' Did she sound as if she was begging? She just wanted to comfort him, nothing else.

'I don't know…'

'Stay. Please. I'd like you to.' She didn't think he should be alone tonight. He'd be feeling all kinds of mixed emotions and needed a distraction from his dark thoughts. She could offer him that distraction. Or they could just sleep and find comfort in not being alone.

They stood up and Noah wrapped his arms around her and hugged her tight. She could feel the need in him as he held her against him. Not just the physical, although that was evident, but the emotional. Noah hadn't allowed himself to give in to his emotional needs because he was afraid of getting too close to someone. But he needed to be loved, cared for and cherished, as everyone did.

CHAPTER TWENTY-THREE

Scarlett woke the next morning from a deep sleep. She'd been dreaming about babies, all yelling to be fed. Candy was trying to get milk out of Puffing Billy to feed them with. Maria was telling her not to use dairy, they weren't baby cows. Dot was sitting on a chair in the middle of the cake shop and laughing, her dog, Crazy Boy, was running around in circles barking.

She'd always had bizarre dreams. In her mid-teens she'd kept a dream diary and had read books about dream interpretation. But none of the things they described were in her dreams. Hers were strange—the ordinary mixed with the extraordinary.

She knew, from her psychiatric nurse training, that we all need to dream, it was the brain's way of making sense of the experiences of the day. She just wished her dreams were more like everyone else's. Why couldn't she dream about Tom Hiddleston for instance?

Not wanting to disturb the sleeping Noah, she lay as still as possible. Last night had been magical. They'd made love for hours, taking their time, neither wanting it to end. Their bodies were becoming familiar, even though they'd only spent the night together twice. It was still new and exciting whilst being comfortable and feeling right.

Miranda had come home in the early hours, so would probably stay in bed until noon. They had plenty of time to be alone.

Scarlett thought about Noah believing he was to blame for his friend's death. How easy it is for people to blame themselves for things that weren't their fault. As if the heart-wrenching pain of losing someone you love isn't bad enough, people then go on to exacerbate that pain by blaming themselves. First Esme and now Noah.

Scarlett carefully crept out of bed and went downstairs. She intended to spoil Noah and shower him with love. It must have taken a lot for him to tell her about Dom. To travel back in time and relive the grief and blame. Guilt was such a pernicious emotion.

And she'd start by making him breakfast in bed. He only ate toast and coffee in the morning, so there wouldn't be much cooking involved.

She made two coffees and a plate of buttered toast and carried them back upstairs.

Noah was awake and yawning. His hair stuck up and he needed a shave but Scarlett would have been happy to stand and watch him all day. Things would be different now between them. No more secrets.

'That smells good,' he said.

Scarlett put the tray on the bed and sat next to it cross-legged. Noah sipped his coffee.

'Did you sleep well?' Scarlett asked.

'Always do when I'm with you,' he said huskily. His words warmed her from the inside out.

'Got any plans for today?' Scarlett asked.

'No, not really. Have you?'

'Thought I might go round to Mum's and see if they've counted the takings yet.'

'Good idea.' Noah finished his coffee. 'Mind if I get a shower?'

'No, of course not.'

After Noah had showered, he realised his phone was almost out of charge. Maybe he could borrow Scarlett's. The bedroom was empty, she must be downstairs. He was just about to shout down to her when he heard her voice. She was on the phone.

He always kept his charger in his bedside cabinet. Perhaps Scarlett did too. He opened the drawer but there was no charger there. There was, however, something else he hadn't expected to see. He took it out and examined it. The box was intact. A pregnancy testing kit. He stared at it as if he couldn't believe what he was looking at.

Did Scarlett think she was pregnant? Why hadn't she done the test? It couldn't belong to anyone else. Why hadn't she told him? He should move. Go downstairs. Ask her about it. But he sat on the bed and stared into space. He raked a hand through his hair. His world shifted as if the view he was familiar with had suddenly changed, revealing things he didn't know were there. How would he feel if Scarlett was pregnant?

They'd used protection but it was never one hundred percent safe. Had they used it every time? He couldn't remember.

He thought about Joel and the joy he and Esme had shown when they'd told everyone that they were expecting. Esme had conceived whilst on honeymoon. They hadn't wanted to wait for their family. Joel was ecstatic at the thought of being a dad. He said he was longing to hold his baby in his arms.

Noah imagined the feeling of a new born baby lying in his arms, sleeping peacefully. That perfect skin that hadn't yet been touch by the world. The softness, the scent. Being prepared to fight dragons to protect them. How did that fit in with his determination to stop people getting close? It didn't. That was someone else's dream, not his. He'd never be a father.

Unless… what if Scarlett was pregnant with his child? What then? Scarlett had broken down his defences, leaving him vulnerable to heartache. She'd paved the way for thoughts he didn't allow himself to have. But a baby… that was a game changer.

He went down the stairs, clutching the box. As soon as he entered the kitchen, Scarlett turned to him with a smile. 'I just spoke to Mum and she says…'

He held the pregnancy testing kit out to her. She looked at him, then the box, then back at his face. The silence stretched out into minutes.

'Scarlett?' He put the box on the table.

'Yes, it's mine. My period's late.' She turned away and took the milk out of the fridge.

'Why haven't you done the test yet?' He wished she'd turn round and look at him. His heart was beating erratically and his mouth was dry as sand.

'I've been putting it off.'

'Why?' His voice came out as a croak. He took a deep breath to calm down.

'I was hoping I wouldn't need it.' Her voice was quiet and she wouldn't look at him. She was obviously feeling as conflicted as he was.

'Don't you think you should do the test?' She turned around then and her face was pale and devoid of make-up. Her freckles stood out in her milky skin.

'Yes, I will. I promise.' She turned away as if the subject was closed, tossing her hair over her shoulders in defiance. But it was far from closed.

'Do it now.' He couldn't wait. He had to know if she was carrying his baby.

'What? Right now?' She looked panicked.

'Yes. Right now. I'll wait.'

Scarlett walked upstairs leaving Noah alone in the kitchen. She went into the bathroom and sat on the toilet. She read the instructions twice because her brain wasn't taking in the information. Her future could possibly depend on the results of her peeing on a white stick.

It was ironic how some of the important events in life were determined by examining some body fluid or other. Usually urine. It could tell the doctors whether a patient had diabetes, blood which could indicate cancer, and of course pregnancy...

Scarlett rested her head in her hands. For goodness sake, do the bloody test! Why was she stalling? Just do it. Now. So she did. More waiting.

Noah's slow footsteps on the stairs made her wonder what he was thinking now. Was he ambivalent as she was, about the result? Did he see fatherhood in his future? With her or someone else? Or was he still refusing to consider it?

Scarlett stood up and paced the short distance from the toilet to the door and back. She'd never felt tension like it. She felt as if she was spinning down a dark tunnel and wondered if she was about to faint.

She'd given it enough time.

She picked the stick up.

Noah didn't know what to think. Why had she put off doing the test? Surely it would set her mind at rest. It wasn't like her. She was usually decisive, especially concerning important things.

Why hadn't she told him? Discussed it with him, shared her feelings? The cynic in him thought she hid it from him because she wanted to decide on her own whether or not to keep the baby. No, that wasn't Scarlett. She would never keep something as vital as this secret. Scarlett had a strong moral compass and she would have told him.

If she was pregnant, he'd support her, co-parent, help her financially. If that was what she wanted. Or maybe she'd agree to live with him. They would be a family, the three of them.

Noah pictured a new-born in a cot next to their bed. A mobile over the cot. The words unconditional love kept moving through his mind. Was he capable of loving a baby enough? A tiny scrap of life that depended on him and Scarlett for everything. He had no doubts about Scarlett. She would take to motherhood like a duck to water, he was sure. But could he step up and be a good father? Yes… he would rise to the challenge and be the best father he could be. The baby would be surrounded by love, growing up with their cousin, Joel and Esme's first child. They'd start school together and play together. As for himself, he'd be part of a loving family. Never be alone anymore.

He was sitting at the top of the stairs. The bathroom door was still firmly closed. He couldn't hear any sound coming from inside. What was she doing in there? How long did it take to do this test?

He stood up when he heard the bathroom door open. Scarlett appeared holding the white stick.

CHAPTER TWENTY-FOUR

'False alarm. I'm not pregnant.'

They stared at each other and for a moment the disappointment was so overwhelming that it rendered him speechless. He wasn't going to be a dad after all. He'd be an uncle to Joel and Esme's kids. He'd never hold his own baby in his arms.

'That's a relief then,' said Scarlett watching him hopefully. 'Panic over.' She laughed nervously.

'Yes, absolutely.'

He didn't know what to say, how to feel, how to make sense of the aching void that had opened up inside him. He hadn't wanted Scarlett to be pregnant had he? He didn't want commitment, responsibility, children.

'Do you want a coffee?' Scarlett asked.

'No thanks.' He wanted to go back in time ten minutes or so when Scarlett came out of the bathroom and for her to tell him he was going to be a dad. They would have worked it out somehow.

Whatever doubts she had, they could have sorted out between them. He had built a future for them in his mind and a little white stick had smashed it to pieces like a wrecking ball demolished a house so there was nothing left but rubble and dust. He needed to be on his own.

'I think I'll shoot off.' He needed the gym to run off his conflicting feelings, to regain his equilibrium, to get back to normal.

'Oh… okay then. I'll go over to Mum's.'

'Right. See you tomorrow then.'

'Yes. See you tomorrow.'

He left without hugging or kissing her. He had to get out.

Scarlett watched him go, running lightly down the stairs. She heard the door slam and then nothing. Silence. She collapsed onto the stair still holding the white stick. Had she just experienced the end of something? A special something that she'd welcomed, felt good about and wanted more of?

A feeling of loneliness dragged her down as she thought of how quickly Noah had left. He couldn't wait to get away. He hadn't even stayed to talk about it. He could have asked her how she felt. He didn't seem to care.

What to do now? Garden? Clean? Cry? Miranda was still in bed so she couldn't even talk to her.

She threw the white stick into the bin in the bathroom, changed into her PJ's and crawled into bed. She buried her head in the pillow that smelled of Noah and pulled the duvet over her.

She waited for the tears to fall, but they were taking their time. She felt blocked as if her body had seized up. Her tear ducts had obviously not got the memo from the brain that it was their turn to do some work. This thought made her giggle which swiftly turned into a sob. One sob led to another and she was gone.

She cried loud, ugly crying that ripped through her body like a fever. Once the floodgates had opened, she had no control over the waves of grief that washed over her.

Once the weeping was over, leaving her exhausted and spent, she wished sleep would come. Nature's healer. Before she could drop off, she heard the front door close. Maria was back from Mum's. Her footsteps crept up the stairs and stopped outside her bedroom.

'Scarlett?'

'Come in.'

'Hi… Oh, what's up? Aren't you well? Where's Noah?'

'He's gone. I'm feeling sorry for myself.'

'You've been crying.'

'Yes, but I've stopped now and I'm not going to cry again.' Maria climbed onto the bed and sat cross-legged, facing Scarlett.

'Tell me. If you want to. It might help.'

So she did. She told Maria everything. From thinking she might be pregnant to Noah's hurried exit. Afterwards, Maria hugged her and then told her how sorry she was that she was in pain like this.

'Maybe, when the dust settles, you should talk to Noah. Have a heart to heart and tell him exactly how you feel.'

Scarlett nodded. But she didn't know if she'd have the strength.

'Do you love him?' Maria asked gently.

'Yes. But he doesn't feel the same way.' Why else would he have left as if he couldn't get away fast enough?

Noah pounded the treadmill. He needed the agony of a long, hard session to sort his head out and heal the crippling pain in his soul.

Noah turned the incline up and increased the speed. He immediately felt the pull in his muscles and powered on until the sweat poured off him and his vision began to blur.

He stopped the treadmill and waited until his gasping breath slowed down to a normal rhythm before taking a long drink of water from his bottle. He felt marginally better, but knew that it would only take one thought to send him back to the black pit of despair.

After showering he headed home. He felt hungry after his strenuous exercise.

'I've saved you some lunch. Lasagne. Shall I warm it up?' asked Esme.

'That'd be great, thanks. Where's Joel?'

'He's gone out for a lunchtime drink with Jon and Hamid. He's going to tell them about the baby. He couldn't wait until he was back at work. There's never much time to talk in the medical centre. He's so excited.'

'It's exciting news. I'm really happy for you both.' Noah pushed the image of babies out of his mind. He concentrated on the wonderful aromas emanating from the dish of lasagne. His stomach rumbled in response.

When it was ready, he sat at the kitchen table to eat it. Esme sat opposite and watched him eat. She liked to see people enjoying the food she'd cooked.

'This is the best lasagne I've ever tasted,' he said. Not a lie, it really was.

'Thanks. It's Scarlett's favourite as well.'

At the mention of Scarlett he felt the band of pain around his heart squeeze a little tighter.

'I hate to see two people I care about in so much emotional turmoil. I want to help, Noah. I had the love and support of my family and friends when I needed it the most and now I want to return that favour.' Esme was watching him, resting her chin on her hand. A look that invited confidences.

He swallowed the last mouthful of food and sat back in his chair.

'I don't know what you can do. Scarlett and I want different things.' Had Scarlett told Esme about the pregnancy scare? She'd probably kept quiet seeing that Esme and Joel had proudly announced their own happy event.

'I think Scarlett just wants someone to share her life with. To fall in love with. Don't you want that?' Esme pierced him with her intense brown eyed stare and he wondered what it was he did want.

'Yes, I suppose, but I'm scared of having someone rely on me in case I let them down.' It sounded pathetic to his own ears, so how would Esme take it? He admired and respected her so much he would hate to be the recipient of her scorn.

'Joel told me about Dom. I hope you don't mind, but we don't have secrets from each other and family shouldn't keep any secrets. I learned that to my peril. You need your family, Noah, and I hope you'll honour me by treating me as one of them.'

'Of course, Esme, I do think of you as family. And I respect your good sense. I don't think our circumstances are the same though.'

'I disagree. I wasted ten years of my life because I'd thought I was to blame for my fiancé's death. I'd hate to see you lose your chance to be happy with Scarlett because of something that happened in the past.'

'It wasn't just something, Esme. It was my fault Dom died. I gave him the wrong advice and he took his own life. I will never get over that.' Noah didn't want to bring it all up again. He'd been put through the wringer recently and he couldn't cope with any more pain.

'Shall I tell you why I think we are alike?'

'Please do.' He smiled to show he wanted to hear what she had to say.

'Because we both thought that we didn't deserve to be happy. I wore sackcloth and ashes for ten long years. You're still wearing them for Dom. But nobody else blames us for what happened. I'm not a psychiatrist, Noah, like you, but I know that I used David's death to hide. From the world, from taking risks, from being happy, and from falling in love. All I can say is that I'm so grateful that your baby brother wouldn't take no for an answer.' Esme smiled and Noah realised, once again, why Joel loved this woman so much.

'Esme, I need your help. I'm out of my depth and don't know which way to turn. I've never felt this way before. I can't live without her but I don't know how to keep her. Will you help me, please?'

'Just answer me one question first. Do you love her?'

Did he love her? That was a question he'd avoided thinking about as he knew he didn't want to let her down. But he had to be honest with Esme, she could see through the barriers he had erected against the world. Barriers that were slowly being knocked down. 'Yes, I love her. With every fibre of my being. With all I am; alcoholic, lonely man who isn't fit to kiss the hem of her dress—or whatever that expression is.'

'Then you need to tell her. It's as hard and as simple as that.'

CHAPTER TWENTY-FIVE

E sme had been right, he needed to talk to Scarlett. But there was something he had to do first.

Telling Scarlett about Dom had brought back memories that Noah didn't want to have. He'd relived it again, his heart breaking for his friend all over again. He'd felt the guilt, the shame, the relentless pain of knowing it had been his fault his friend had taken his own life.

There was another guilt tugging at him with its sharp claws. He hadn't seen Dom's parents for years. At first, after the funeral, they'd stayed in touch with phone calls, letters, the occasional visit. They'd sent Christmas cards with short messages, wishing each other well. On the anniversary of his death Noah had phoned Dom's parents and they'd made polite, desultory conversation. A ritual, born out of guilt and remorse.

Maybe talking to them would help him. They'd never really spoken about what had happened or given each other the chance to express their feelings. He had never said he was sorry or told them it was his fault. He hadn't wanted to add to their pain. Or perhaps he was just too much of a coward.

He had to make amends, for his sake as much as theirs. They deserved to know the truth.

Noah phoned Frank and Elsie to ask if he could visit. They had been overjoyed to hear from him which made him feel worse. They insisted he stay the night. He could have got to Cardiff and back in one day but he owed them and agreed to stay.

They were waiting for him when he pulled up on their driveway and Elsie cried as she hugged him.

'It's lovely to see you, Noah. We talk about you a lot, don't we Frank?'

'We do. Come inside.'

Their conversation at first was about the weather, the journey, and how well he was looking. They asked about the hospital and whether he liked psychiatry. Elsie made tea and brought it into the neat living-room with a plate of biscuits.

The room was rather old-fashioned with a heavily patterned carpet, a solid dark wood sideboard on which sat an array of framed photos. One of their wedding day, another of the three of them when Dom was a child and the rest of Dom at various ages. He was their only child and they doted on him.

Suddenly Noah wanted to leave. Why had he come? He had no right to be here with this bereaved couple still grieving the death of their son. What right did he have to make their suffering worse, just so he could feel better about himself?

'Why now, Noah?' asked Frank quietly. 'Not that we're not pleased to see you because we are. But we've not seen you for over ten years. Why now?'

'I need to tell you something.' He hoped it didn't end the tenuous link that he had with Dom. None of them would ever forget him.

'About Dom?' asked Elsie.

'Yes. He asked for my advice when he felt overwhelmed with being a medical student. He wanted to leave. Said he wasn't cut out for being a doctor. And I told him not to give up.' Frank and Elsie were listening carefully and sipping their tea. He studied them, watching for signs of the effect his words were having on them. He felt slightly sick at the confession he was about to make. 'I gave him wrong advice. It was my fault. I told him how disappointed you would be. How proud you were of him, the first doctor in the family, and how he needed to stay and finish his training. He was relying on me to give him the right advice but I failed him. He died because of me.'

He wanted to put his head in his hands and hide from them, but he forced himself to look them in the eye. Which is why he saw the puzzled look pass between them.

'And you've spent all these years thinking it was your fault?' asked Frank.

'Because it was.' He owned it. It was his mistake and he wasn't going to be persuaded otherwise, no matter how kindly meant.

'No, lad, it wasn't. I knew all about that. Dom rang us that night. He told me he was coming home. But I had to give him some bad news. That's why he took his own life, it wasn't you. It was me.'

'What news?' Noah couldn't believe what he was hearing. They knew he was coming home. The words rang in his head like discordant bells.

'Did he ever mention Gwyneth?' asked Elsie.

'He might have done.' Noah searched his memory but came up with nothing.

'She was his childhood sweetheart. He was mad about her. We thought she felt the same, but…' Frank was visibly upset and Noah felt slightly sick.

'She married someone else,' said Elsie.

'I had to tell him if he was coming home. I couldn't let him think she was still in love with him. I was trying to protect him, see, but I sent him to his grave.' Frank broke down and wept. He put his head in his hands.

Elsie sat next to him and put her arms around him rocking him like a baby.

'There now, don't blame yourself. You did what you thought was right.'

Noah looked on helplessly. He'd caused this. Opened up old wounds that would never fully heal. Caused two people who didn't deserve it, pain and anguish. It was never far from the surface when parents had lost a child.

But the implications for him were immense. Dom was on his way home. He'd ignored his advice and had made his own decision. He was going to leave anyway.

As Noah watched Elsie comforting her husband he thought about Dom, seeing his friend clearly in his mind's eye. Then his psychiatric training kicked in and he realised there were questions that needed answering. Suicide was rarely caused by just one thing. There were so many factors to consider. Noah had looked after too many patients who had suicidal thoughts as a result of a mental health problem they were struggling with. Celine was a perfect example. She'd had a miscarriage that led to heavy drinking that, in turn, led to one suicide attempt. Was this also the case for Dom?

He felt stupid now not realising the complexity of feelings in someone thinking of taking their own life. As if something he'd said as a clueless medical student could have carried that much weight. How arrogant was he to think his opinion would push someone to end their life? And why hadn't he known about Gwyneth? Dom must have mentioned her if she'd meant that much to him.

Frank had recovered from his crying jag and he and Elsie were sitting next to each other, holding hands.

'Can I ask you something?' He was thinking more clearly now. Trying to look at Dom as one of his patients and following the mental processes that would lead to a correct diagnosis.

'Of course,' said Frank.

'Did Dom suffer from depression?'

'Yes, love, he did,' said Elsie. It started in high school but he had it on and off for a few years. He had help but he didn't want anyone to know about it when he went to medical school.'

'Had he ever mentioned suicide, or attempted to take his life before?' Noah was aware that these questions could cause this lovely couple more pain, but now he was here, he was determined to get to the bottom of Dom's death.

'Well... there was a time when he was in the sixth form that he took an over dose. He told us it was an accident as he was on antidepressives, but I always had a feeling there was more to it than that,' said Elsie.

It was clear to Noah now. Dom had suffered from depression and medical school had made that worse. Then the news about Gwyneth may have been the last straw. There might have been other things that contributed but they would never know now.

'What are you thinking, son?' asked Frank. Noah realised he had been quiet for a while.

'There's a high rate of suicide among medical students. So many different reasons why someone might choose that way out. I can imagine how tempting it is. I used alcohol, other students, like Dom, see suicide as a way out. I remember the shame I felt when I failed an exam. I thought I wasn't good enough to be a doctor. It took a tremendous amount of effort to make me stay and I worked so hard to get the right grade. And I never suffered from depression as Dom did.'

'So, what are you saying?' asked Frank with a frown.

'I'm saying that it wasn't your fault or mine, although I still feel guilty about not realising he was suffering from depression. I should have done more, supported him…'

'You were a good friend to Dom,' said Elsie tearfully, 'he was always saying how much you did for him.'

'It wasn't enough though, was it?'

The time for beating themselves up was over. They all needed to lay Dom to rest.

Scarlett got out of bed and dressed in jeans and a T-shirt. The crying had helped but talking to Maria had been better. Her sister was the strength she needed.

She had to get away from the house, and from Leytonsfield, just for a few hours. When she'd passed her driving test and had bought her first car—a Mini—she'd often taken the car out and driven around the Cheshire countryside. Then when she'd become braver, she'd taken the car on the motorways. She loved the speed of the fast lane. It had been exhilarating and she had often pushed the car to the max even to the point of breaking the speed limit. Everyone in the fast lane drove too fast and she was no exception. Surprisingly, she'd never had a speeding ticket.

She needed that now. To just get in her car and drive.

'I'm going out, Maria,' she shouted as she opened the front door. Maria was in the living-room, reading. She poked her head around the door.

'Where are you going? Do you feel better now? Do you want me to come?'

'I'm going for a drive and have no idea where I'll end up. I do feel better after our talk, thanks. No, I want to be alone, but thanks for all your support. You're an angel.'

Maria didn't look convinced. 'Drive carefully won't you?'

'Always.' She left the house.

She loved driving her Audi. She'd had several cars since the Mini and the Audi was the best. Okay, it wasn't a Ford Mustang, her most favourite car in all the world, but it was powerful and responsive.

As Scarlett drove towards the motorway, she thought of the present she'd given Noah for his birthday. He would get to drive his Lamborghini, and she had been the one to make it happen. She didn't want to think about Noah. She still didn't know why he had left her house so abruptly when he had found out she wasn't pregnant. It was rude and cruel. He should have asked her how she felt about it. At least stayed long enough to make sure she was okay. It was a big thing, thinking you were pregnant and then finding you weren't. They should have talked it through. But he shot out of the door like a cork out of a bottle.

They had used contraception the night they'd made love, but not the following morning. She had been half asleep; it always took her a while to come round. She slept deeply and took a long time to wake up.

She joined the motorway and soon moved into the fast lane. It was busy, lots of cars out for a Sunday drive. Unlike her though they probably all had a destination in mind.

Her thoughts drifted back to Noah and the pregnancy that wasn't. Maybe Noah saw it as too close a call. She could have been pregnant. And in fact, she had thought she was. She felt different. And no… she couldn't explain that to herself or anyone else. It would have been nice, if Noah had reacted differently, being pregnant at the same time as Esme. Sharing pregnancy stories, growing big and fat.

And then, when the babies were born, they would grow up together. Two little cousins who became inseparable. They would go to the same nursery, the same school and… and she had to stop thinking like that. She wasn't pregnant, and she was glad she wasn't.

Noah hadn't stayed to support her, so he obviously had no real feelings for her.

There was only one thing to do. She needed to talk to him. Now. Demand to know why he ran out like that. She hadn't deserved such treatment. She wasn't going to rest until she'd talked it out. And if it meant the end of them, then so be it. She'd accept the relationship that never was the same way she had accepted the pregnancy that never was. She'd move on with her life and go back to the way things were. Before Noah became part of the family. Before Joel and Esme fell in love. Before Noah became more than the consultant in charge of the unit. Before… before she gave her heart to him, even if he hadn't realised that was what she'd done.

But the first thing she needed to do was turn around and head back to Leytonsfield.

Scarlett moved into the slow lane and waited for the slip road to exit the motorway. There was more traffic on this lane and it was moving too slowly for Scarlett's liking. Music, that would distract her. As she pressed buttons to get to a playlist she wanted, she rehearsed in her mind what she would say to Noah. Why did he run out on her for a start.

She'd taken her eyes off the road for a second so hadn't noticed that the car in front had slowed down considerably. As the car loomed closer to hers she slammed on the brakes and just stopped in time to prevent her car crashing into the back of it. Unfortunately, the driver behind didn't have Scarlett's fast reflexes and went into the back of her car which shunted her into the one in front. The two crashes, one after the other, shook Scarlett so much that she nearly saw stars.

It all happened so fast. The airbag inflated, car horns started blaring, people were shouting and Scarlett felt dizzy. Then gradually all noises receded into the distance and a buzzing in her ears was the last thing she heard as the world turned black.

CHAPTER TWENTY-SIX

S carlett woke up when her mother's voice penetrated the fog her brain had been drifting in.

'Scarlett, open your eyes for me. That's it. You're in hospital, darling, you've been in an accident. Can you speak?' She tried but no sound came out. 'Never mind, sweetheart, the doctor is going to give you something for the pain. You'll be alright now. Maria is here.'

Maria was crying but she held her hand which comforted Scarlett. She had no idea what was going on. Her neck felt as though someone had tried to screw it off her shoulders. She'd never felt pain like it. Then she thought she felt a needle in her hand but she couldn't lift her head to see. Then it all went black again.

· ♥ · ♥ · ♥ · ♥ · ♥ ·

Noah left Frank and Elsie's with promises to visit more often. They stood on the pavement with their arms around each other and waved as he left. He watched them in the rear-view mirror until he turned off their road and headed for the motorway.

He sighed deeply. The news about Dom not taking any notice of his advice should have made him feel better. It hadn't been his fault. After all the years of thinking he was to blame, he should feel the weight of guilt lift from his shoulders.

But he didn't.

He had lived with the guilt feelings for so long that they had become part of who he was. The alcoholic who had been responsible for his friend's death. That was how he saw himself. That was who he had been. Now he had to think of himself in a different way. He wasn't that man, so who was he? All he felt at that moment was empty.

And poor Frank and Elsie, thinking they had been to blame, by having to tell Dom that Gwyneth had married someone else. And poor Dom, suffering from clinical depression, trying to cope with the overwhelming pressures and stresses of being a trainee doctor. Treating patients while suffering himself.

We are all responsible for our own actions. Taking control of your life was empowering. We all have narratives we tell ourselves. All these thoughts floated in and out of his mind. Not very helpful. Because it wasn't what happened to you in life, it was how you reacted to it. It was how you felt that counted.

Noah realised that if he thought about it anymore he'd give himself a headache. He was eager to get home now and talk to Scarlett. He needed to explain his reaction when he'd forced her to do the pregnancy test. She hadn't been ready and he shouldn't have bullied her.

He wanted to phone her but had forgotten to charge his phone before he left for Cardiff and it was now as flat as a pancake. In a way it was quite liberating to be off grid. No one could contact him. In another way he was suffering from FOMO—fear of missing out.

What was going on back home? He'd only been away one night and he felt as if it was weeks. Perhaps he needed a holiday. But first, he had to talk to Scarlett. He wouldn't let her down. He hadn't let Dom down. The only person he'd let down was himself.

He joined the motorway and headed for home.

The last thing he expected when he arrived home was an empty house.

There was a message from Joel that chilled the blood in his veins and he had to sit down before he collapsed.

"Tried to ring you. Scarlett is in Leytonsfield A&E. Candy, Esme and I are with her. Not life-threatening."

Not life-threatening. Noah was glad Joel had included that. But why was she in A&E?

He got back in his car and drove to the hospital, his heart thudding, a sick feeling in his stomach. He tried not to panic but felt it there just beneath the surface. He fought the feelings of dread that clouded his mind. Not life-threatening. He needed to hold on to that thought and not assume anything. Why hadn't he charged his phone? Although he couldn't have got back from Cardiff any quicker. He had made good time and was anticipating a long shower and a hot meal.

But instead…

When he arrived, he parked in his usual place and ran all the way to the A&E department. It was mad busy as usual but being a consultant had its advantages and he grabbed the first doctor he saw and was directed to Scarlett's cubicle.

'Noah! Thank goodness. We tried to ring…' Joel looked relieved to see him.

Scarlett was lying still with a neck brace on. She was pale and the area around her eyes looked bruised. Probably from the airbag. She didn't look conscious.

'What happened?'

'I think it looks worse than it is, Noah,' said Esme. 'She's been given a strong pain killer and she keeps falling asleep.'

He bent over her and stroked her face. 'Scarlett?' There was no response, so he turned to Joel. 'How did it happen?'

'She was driving on a motorway and someone went into the back of her which shunted her car into the one in front. She was lucky really as she wasn't driving very fast.'

'Where was she going?' Noah turned to Candy.

'Maria said she just wanted to go for a drive. She loves driving. But fortunately she wasn't in the fast lane or it would have been so much worse.'

'What did the doctor say?'

'Whiplash and bruising to her face caused by the airbag. They're waiting for a bed on a ward.' Joel spoke quietly and Noah was grateful for his calm efficiency. He was a good man to have around in an emergency.

'I think I need to sit down.' He collapsed onto a plastic chair and put his head in his hands. It had all been too much. The news about Dom and now Scarlett in an accident.

'Are you alright, darling?' asked Candy who put her hand on his shoulder and gave it a rub. He was grateful for the physical contact. He felt quite emotional suddenly.

'Yes. Sorry, it's been quite a day.'

The doctor looking after her stuck his head in and said they were taking her up to a ward now and she needed to rest so it would be better if they came back tomorrow. Noah knew it wouldn't benefit Scarlett to have her family around her while she was sleeping and they would only get in the way of the nursing staff.

He kissed Scarlett on her forehead. 'I'll come back tomorrow,' he whispered.

Scarlett awoke on the ward, in a four-bed bay. The memories of the previous day were hazy, but one thing stayed in her mind as clear as spring water. She'd had a scan to make sure there were no internal injuries and a blood test. Her vital signs were being monitored regularly.

The doctor on the ward had come to talk to her before breakfast. When he'd left she couldn't eat a thing.

Candy was the first person to visit her. She walked onto the ward like a member of the royal family on a tour. Except for the bouquet of flowers and the large box of fruit she carried. Her pastel blue trouser suit and snow white blouse matched her immaculate blonde bob and perfectly applied make-up. She looked as regal as ever.

'Darling,' she cried as she found the right bed. 'You look better than you did last night. How are you feeling?'

'A bit better.' She pointed to her foam collar. 'Does this suit me, do you think? Maybe I'll keep it as a fashion accessory.'

'Sweetheart, it's only for a couple of days. That's what that nice young doctor said, isn't it?' Candy put the flowers and fruit on top of the cabinet next to the bed.

'You mean the one who looked as if he'd just finished his A levels? Yes, he did say that. It's a sign of old age you know when you think the doctors are looking younger. And policemen and women.'

'You're not old, you're still a young woman.' Candy perched on the side of the bed and took Scarlett's hand.

'I know. I meant you.'

'Oh ha ha. Good to see you've not lost your sense of humour.'

'Well, they say it's the last to go. Or is that hearing?'

Her mum stroked her hair back from her face. 'How are you really feeling, Scarlett?'

Time to get serious. 'Mum, I need to tell you something.'

Her mum frowned and studied her face. 'Is it something the doctor told you?' She nodded, then regretted the action as she got a shooting pain in her neck. There was no more joking now. It was serious. When she didn't smile or crack a joke, her mum put her hand to her mouth. 'Oh no, is it serious? Are you ill? Is it bad? Oh, Scarlett, just tell me.'

'It's not bad.' She smiled to put her mum at ease.

'Thank goodness. So what is it?' Scarlett waited for her mother to guess. Seconds went by and Scarlett amused herself by watching the changing emotions flicker across her mother's face. Worry expressed by a frown. Going through the options in her mind followed by a great big grin when the penny dropped. 'You're pregnant! Is that it? How wonderful.'

Scarlett smiled even though she didn't think it could be described as wonderful.

'Please don't tell anyone, not until I've told Noah. I need to tell him first.'

'Of course, darling. I won't say a word. Does anyone know?'

'I did a test on the open day. Noah found the testing kit and pushed me into doing it. It was negative. But now I've got to tell him that there's been a mistake and actually I am pregnant. I'm not looking forward to that one bit.'

'But he'll be delighted, surely?' Her mother couldn't imagine anyone not being delighted at baby news.

'Not if last time is anything to go by. He couldn't get away fast enough.' Scarlett closed her eyes and tried not to think of Noah fleeing the house.

'When he thought it was negative? Maybe he wants to be a father. He could have been disappointed.'

'No, Mum. He doesn't want to be a father. He doesn't want responsibility, commitment and he certainly doesn't want me.' To her dismay she burst into tears.

'Darling, don't cry.' Candy wrapped her arms around Scarlett who clung to her as if she was drowning. 'Everything will be fine, you'll see.'

CHAPTER TWENTY-SEVEN

After lunch, Scarlett had more visitors. Miranda and Ashley appeared just as Scarlett was settling down for a short nap.

'Hi,' Miranda sing-songed as she sat on the edge of the bed. Ashley followed her carrying a huge bag of fruit.

'Hi. This is a nice surprise. Thanks for coming.'

'We wanted to come straight away, didn't we, Ash? When we heard you'd been in an accident. You poor thing. However did it happen?'

Miranda took the grapes out of the bag and was eating them whilst waiting for Scarlett to tell her all about it. Ashley sat in a chair at the side of the bed.

'I was on the motorway...' Scarlett recounted the story again wondering how many more times she'd have to repeat it. It was obviously her fault and sounded worse with each telling.

'Are you badly injured? The neck brace... '

'No. I can take it off in a couple of days and the doctor thinks I might be able to go home tomorrow.'

'That's fantastic! Good news. I was so worried, wasn't I, Ash?'

'Yep.' Ashley grinned at her.

'Are you going to your mum's so she can look after you?'

'I wasn't going to. I should be okay in a few days.'

'I think you should. In fact, I know you should. You'll be alone when Maria and I are at work.'

'I'll be okay.'

Miranda looked at Ashley who was scrolling on his phone. 'Ash? You couldn't be a sweetie and see if there's a drinks machine? Three teas?' She fluttered her eyelashes at him.

'Okay.' He hauled himself off the chair and wandered down the ward.

'Has Noah been to see you yet?'

'He's coming later. Why?' Scarlett wondered why Miranda would ask about Noah. It was obvious she was loved-up with Ashley.

Miranda frowned and lowered her voice. 'Have you told him?'

'Have I told him what?' Scarlett was tired and finding it hard to keep her eyes open. But she sprung awake at Miranda's next question.

'That you're not pregnant. I found the pregnancy testing stick in the bin in the bathroom and it was negative. I imagine you're relieved but a little bit disappointed?'

'Can you keep a secret?' She'd have to tell her now. The more people she told the more real it became.

'Of course. Pinkie promise.' She offered Scarlett her little finger and she obliged.

'They did a scan yesterday and I am pregnant. That first test was a false negative. Which was all Noah's fault for rushing her.

'Oh my, you're having a baby. How lovely. That's such good news.' Miranda beamed with pleasure.

'Yes, of course it is.' Scarlett couldn't imagine why Miranda thought it was good news.

'It makes my news a bit easier to tell you. Ashley wants me to move in with him. So I'll be moving out. I'm sorry if it causes you any inconvenience but now you're pregnant you and Noah will be an item and I'll be able to pay back the money he gave me and—'

'Why did he give you money?'

'I probably shouldn't have mentioned that. I couldn't pay you for the rent and the deposit so I asked for an advance on my salary. But Noah gave me the money himself. Wasn't that kind of him? And he took me to Pizza First. He is such a lovely man, you are so lucky.'

Why would Noah have given Miranda the money for the rent and why hadn't he told her?

'There was a time I thought you fancied him.' Scarlett was tired now and wanted to be alone to think. But Miranda looked quite happy sitting on the bed eating grapes. Ashley was obviously having trouble finding the drinks machine.

'You're right, I did. Until I realised that he only had eyes for one woman.'

'Who's that?' Scarlett asked sleepily. She didn't think she could keep her eyes open for much longer.

'You, you idiot. He has always loved you, you know.'

When Scarlett woke it was late afternoon and her visitors had gone.

She struggled up and pottered to the bathroom. She looked a mess. The skin around her eyes were a strange blend of purple, green and yellow. Quite a nice colour palette, but not under her eyes. She looked awful.

She used the loo, had a wash and tried to comb her hair. What does it matter, she thought and went back to bed. Before she clambered in she noticed an envelope on the top of the bedside cabinet. The flowers were now in a vase and the fruit bowl stood beside it.

There was a note in the envelope saying, *"Just a little token from me and Ashley for when you've recovered. You're a very special person, Scarlett, and I'm so glad we're friends."* She took out a voucher for a spa weekend for two. What a lovely thought. She had changed her mind about Miranda and now knew her to be a kind person. A little over the top, but genuine, nonetheless. She sent a quick text thanking her for the voucher.

There was a text message from Noah to tell her that he would see her as soon as he finished work. She ignored it.

She lay in bed and thought about everything that had happened over the last few days. Noah rushing out of the house when he found out she wasn't pregnant. He then went to Cardiff to talk to Dom's parents but he hadn't told her he was going. He just went. He gave Miranda the money for the rent and deposit but didn't bother to tell her he'd done that. And why had he done it? Not for her sake, for Miranda's. Maybe he had wanted to get together with Miranda but she fell for Ashley before he could do anything about it.

He didn't want commitment, responsibility or any kind of relationship. He'd made that plain. It all added up to one thing. He wasn't interested in her in that way. He certainly didn't want her for the long term. But she was pregnant with his baby. A baby he didn't want.

She'd been on the way to talk to him when she crashed. They'd never really talked about their feelings. She had wanted to when she thought she wasn't pregnant. It would have been the perfect time to be honest with each other. But he ran. Left her alone to deal with whatever she was feeling.

So, where did that leave her? If Miranda was moving out they'd either have to find someone else or move back in with Mum, at least until the baby was born. Maria would be happy anyway.

What was happening to her? Her life had changed dramatically in a short time. She admitted to herself that she didn't like all the uncertainty. She could be spontaneous such as when someone said, "Let's go out for the day" or "Fancy going on a pub crawl?" but not "How about getting pregnant to a man who doesn't want you?"

After eating a sandwich for her evening meal as she had no appetite but needed to keep her strength up, she waited for visiting time.

Noah might not be here for ages. He said as soon as he finished work, but knowing Noah, that could be any time after six o'clock.

Scarlett was looking forward to being discharged the following day so she could go home. But which home? Hers and Maria's or Mum's? She hoped Miranda would agree to stay until the end of the month before moving out to live with Ashley. She was right though, Miranda and Maria would be at work and she'd be alone in an empty house.

There was a lot to decide but the first thing she had to do was to tell Noah he was going to be a father. She made a deal with herself. If he was alone when he visited she'd tell him. If there were other people visiting, she wouldn't tell him until she was back home. She owed it to him to give him space when he found out. If his reaction to her not being pregnant was anything to go by, he needed an escape route.

She lay still watching the other patients' visitors arrive. Maybe no one would visit tonight. Then Esme, Joel and Noah appeared and she was so pleased to see them she nearly burst into tears. Was she being a wimp or was it baby hormones?

'Hello darling how are you feeling?' asked Esme.

'Hello trouble,' said Joel kissing her on the forehead.

Noah hung back, looking at her uncertainly. She ignored him. She wasn't sure she'd forgiven him yet for… all kinds of things.

'I realise it could have been worse. I'm looking forward to going home tomorrow.'

'Mum's looking forward to having you at home. Be prepared to be waited on hand and foot,' said Esme with a smile.

'I was thinking of going back to my house with Maria and Miranda.'

'I don't think that's a good idea,' said Joel. 'Let your mum look after you, at least for a week or so. You need rest. Whiplash is a painful condition.'

Noah came forward then and kissed her on the forehead. A brotherly kiss. Is that how he saw her now?

'Hi Noah, how are you?'

'I think I'm probably better than you are. I'm so sorry about the accident. My phone was dead and—'

'It's okay. Joel told me you were in Cardiff.'

'Yes. I'd like to tell you all about it. When you get home tomorrow. And for what it's worth, I agree with Joel. You should let your mum look after you.' Noah smiled at her but it was a bedside manner smile, not a potential partner one. She didn't smile back.

'Looks like it's unanimous,' she said looking at Esme.

'Yes, I agree,' said Esme, 'We were so worried about you. Mum wants you under her roof for a while. It's the best place for you.'

'Okay, I give in. I'll go home.' The thought pleased her. She felt the need for some TLC and her mum was the best person to give it.

Esme perched on the edge of the bed and took her hand. She relished the firm touch and the support that she felt was passing from Esme to her. She was still feeling vulnerable and liable to cry at any moment. And she hadn't even told Noah the news yet.

She realised she had to tell him as soon as she could as it was preventing her from thinking of the baby as a positive thing. All she could focus on was how Noah was going to react. She was trying to protect herself by being prepared for the worst case scenario. But she wanted to feel the joy of impending motherhood, think of all the happy times they would have as a family when the two babies arrived.

The first thing she'd do when she got out of hospital was tell Noah he was going to be a father.

CHAPTER TWENTY-EIGHT

Scarlett woke up at home in her own bed. The one she'd had as a child. She put her hands on her stomach protectively. 'Hi, baby' she said quietly, feeling a warm glow fill her body. She couldn't quite believe she was pregnant even though the doctor had confirmed it.

It was early and Connie would still be in bed. Her mother, though, was eating toast in the kitchen.

'Darling, you don't have to be up at this time. Why don't you stay in bed and rest?'

'Mum, I've just spent two days in bed and I don't need any more rest. I'm bored, I want something to do. How about I help you in the shop for a couple of hours?'

Her mum put her hands on Scarlett's shoulders and examined her face. 'The bruising's better. You could cover the rest with concealer. How's the neck?'

'It's better. I'm not wearing the brace anymore and the doctor said I need to do gentle exercises. I can always do some baking in the back. I'm so bored, I want to do something.'

Why was it that, no matter how old you were, whenever you're back with your mum you revert to being a whiny teenager?

'Okay, you can do a couple of hours. But if you feel the slightest bit sore or tired, you're to come home, okay?'

'Promise.'

Candy wrapped her arms around her and Scarlett gave in to her mother's embrace. She breathed in her perfume and relaxed into her warmth and softness. What kind of mother was she going to make? Thoughts of the new life growing inside her were never far away.

'When are you going to tell Noah about the baby?'

'Next time I see him.'

'And when will that be?'

'Soon.'

'Scarlett, you need to tell him before someone else does. Do it today.'

Scarlett knew her mum was right. She could imagine Miranda congratulating him in her usual exuberant way, before realising he didn't know. It wasn't fair to Noah. She had to tell him but was dreading it. He wasn't going to be happy.

Scarlett enjoyed baking cupcakes and muffins after she had helped Bernice with the breakfasts. It was good to be active again and making herself useful. She'd only been in hospital for two days but those days had felt a lot longer. It must be awful for patients who were bedridden for weeks.

'Scarlett? You've got a visitor.' Her mother's voice broke into her thoughts. A visitor? Who knew she was at Candy Dots?

She was surprised to see Noah standing in the middle of the shop and didn't know how to react. He looked uneasy as if he wasn't sure of the reception he'd get.

'Mum?'

'Now, don't be angry. I texted Noah and asked him to meet you for lunch. You need to talk. I've put some sandwiches and a cupcake each in this bag.'

'Thanks,' said Scarlett.

Noah looked bemused. Maybe it was better this way. She didn't have time to worry and stress about it. She'd just tell him and whatever happened… well, she'd deal with it.

'You're looking better,' said Noah.

'Thanks. Listen, I didn't know anything about this. Mum took it upon herself to bring us together.'

'It's okay. In fact, it's good to get out of the hospital. It's been quite a morning.'

'Oh? I could come back to work, I feel so much better.'

'No. Absolutely not. You need to rest. We'll manage. We always do.'

They wandered down Market Street and sat on a bench to eat their lunch.

'I don't have a lot of time, but your Mum's text hinted at something you wanted to tell me?' Scarlett's sandwich turned to ashes in her mouth. How could she just blurt it out? And in such a public place? 'Scarlett.' Noah's voice had an impatient tone. He was probably desperate to get back to the hospital.

'Yes, sorry. Okay. I did the pregnancy test and it was negative.'

Noah was staring at her with a frown deepening the grooves between his eyebrows. She couldn't stop staring at them.

'Go on,' he said quietly.

'It was a false negative.' There, she'd said it. He was a doctor, he should be able to work it out.

'A false negative, meaning…?'

'The doctor said it could have been caused by one of several things. There weren't enough pregnancy hormones to give an accurate reading, I didn't do the test properly, or the kit was an old one, or…

I don't know, I can't remember everything he said. Anyway, I had a scan, while I was in hospital and I'm pregnant.' She daren't look at him, but when she did, she was amazed. She couldn't believe his reaction.

The frown had vanished to be replaced by a look of wonder, incredulity, joy… Scarlett thought of all the words she could use while waiting for Noah to speak. He had tears in his eyes which she hadn't expected.

'Scarlett, that's wonderful! I'm going to be a dad. I'm really going to be a dad.'

'Yes, you are.' And she was going to be a mother although Noah obviously hadn't thought that far ahead. She breathed a sigh of relief. He didn't seem angry or upset. 'I'm glad you're happy about it.'

'Aren't you? Happy?'

He was actually asking her how she felt. That was a first. Maybe that was unfair. She couldn't rid herself of the memory of him running out of her house after the first pregnancy test.

'I'm still getting used to the idea. It came as a bit of a shock to be honest. I'd just grown used to thinking I wasn't pregnant when I had to do a U-turn and get my head around the fact I was.'

Noah took her hands in his and looked into her eyes. 'I know I have a lot of apologising to do and also a lot of explaining. I've treated you badly and I'm so sorry. Can we talk? I mean really talk? I have so much to say to you. Will you go out with me, Scarlett? For a meal? It'll be our first date and it's long overdue. Tonight?'

Scarlett couldn't believe it. Who was this man and what had he done with Noah? It was as if the normal quiet and sometimes taciturn man had turned into another person altogether. Talkative, falling over his words, tears in his eyes and grinning.

'Yes, Noah, I will go out with you.' She grinned too and he leaned forward and kissed her gently on the lips. A group of school kids walked past wolf whistling and making kissing sounds. They both ignored them.

Their first date. Be still my beating heart, she thought. Then grinned.

Noah was delighted that he had managed to book a table at Rocco's, one of the best Italian restaurants in Leytonsfield, due to a cancellation.

As he got ready, choosing his clothes carefully, he was as excited as a teenager on a first date. He was a thirty-six year old man on a date with the mother of his child. He still couldn't believe he was going to be a father. Every time that thought nudged him and he pictured what he thought their baby would look like, he felt a tingle start inside him and spread out to his whole being. A tingle of delight, awe and a hint of disbelief.

How could it be happening to him? When Scarlett had done the pregnancy test on the open day he'd been desperate for the test to be positive. It would have been a sign that he had been forgiven. Who by he didn't know. The universe? God? He had thought that maybe he was being given a second chance.

Then, when the test had been negative, it had reaffirmed what he had believed for a long time; that he didn't deserve to be happy. What gave him the right to think he'd make a good father after what he'd done?

But now that no longer applied. He hadn't been responsible for Dom's death and he did deserve to be happy. And he was going to be a father! He felt lighter and more optimistic than he'd ever felt in his whole life.

There was only one thing left for him to do. Convince Scarlett that he loved her.

'What are you going to wear?' asked Candy.

'A dress. He said to look smart in his text. I don't have many dresses so… maybe the green one.'

'I think that would be perfect. How are you feeling? About Noah I mean.'

'It's strange. This is what I've wanted—to be going on a date with Noah. But now I've got it I'm not sure how I feel. I thought I'd be happy, ecstatic even, but I can't help thinking about how he just left after pushing me to do the pregnancy test. He didn't even stick around to ask me how I felt.'

'I agree, it doesn't sound like Noah at all. He's such a considerate man. What did you say to him when you found out it was negative?'

'Something about it being a relief I think.'

'That could be the problem. Maybe he thought you didn't want his baby.'

'But it wasn't like that…'

'Listen darling, you need to talk to him. This is your opportunity to clear the air. Tell each other exactly how you're feeling.' Her mother smiled and Scarlett nodded.

'You're right. It's time to be an adult.'

'There's nothing that makes us grow up faster than having a child.'

Scarlett shivered thinking of the responsibility of looking after a baby. At least she wouldn't be alone. She had her mum, Esme who was going through the same process as her, her other sisters and, hopefully, Noah. Provided he could convince her that he wanted her for herself and not just because she was pregnant.

CHAPTER TWENTY-NINE

Rocco's was the height of sophistication. Scarlett felt special being treated to a meal in such a beautiful place. It was all dark wood, shiny candelabras and soft lighting. The aroma of the food cooking—garlic and spices— made her stomach rumble.

'Wow,' Scarlett said, 'this is a treat.'

'Have you eaten here before?' Noah asked. He was wearing his suit trousers and matching waistcoat again and looked devilishly sexy. He smiled warmly at her and seemed relaxed and happy. The frown lines were not as noticeable tonight.

'A couple of times. Usually on special occasions.'

'This is a special occasion, Scarlett. We're celebrating the baby.'

'Just the baby?'

He grinned. 'I'd like to say the beginning of us, but I don't want to be presumptuous. After all, this is only our first date. But I'm hoping it'll be the first of many.'

'You're different tonight. I can't quite put my finger on it…' She studied him but instead of looking embarrassed as he would have done, he grinned and his brown eyes brimmed with tenderness and passion. She stared into their depths and felt she could easily fall in and drown.

A waiter brought the menus. Noah waved away the wine list. 'Two mineral waters please.'

They ordered. Noah ordered steak and Scarlett opted for the chicken. They decided to order a sweet after the mains.

As they sipped their drinks, Scarlett watched him. His eyes were the colour of liquid chocolate and held a promise that made her hot and restless.

She sat back and waited for him to speak, but he seemed happy to sit in silence. This wasn't what they were here for.

'What happened when you went to see Dom's parents?'

'I discovered something that changed my life.'

'Oh?' Scarlett hadn't expected that. 'What?'

'They told me things about Dom that I didn't know. He'd suffered from clinical depression—I feel quite ashamed that I hadn't picked that up—and he hadn't taken my advice not to give up on medicine as he was on his way home to Wales. But his father had to tell him that the woman he loved had married someone else. So his suicide could have been the result of several things.'

'Poor Dom.' At first Scarlett could only think of a poor young man taking his life because he had too many pressures and mental health issues to deal with. Then, the implications for Noah became clear. Why had he thought it was his fault? If only he'd talked it over with Dom's parents at the time he wouldn't have spent all those years blaming himself.

'What are you thinking, Scarlett? You're very quiet.

'I was wondering how different your life will be now. You have no reason to feel that weight of guilt you've been carrying for so long. You have nothing to reproach yourself for. That must be such a relief.'

'It is. Although I still feel I let him down. I should have known he was struggling and talked to him. Helped him more. That guilt is hard to shake. But I have to forget the past now and look to the future. With you and our baby.'

'I need to ask you something, Noah.'

'Okay. Ask away.'

The waiter brought their main course and it gave Scarlett time to think how she was going to word her question.

'When I did the pregnancy test on the open day, why did you leave so abruptly? Why didn't you stay and talk to me?'

'Because I was disappointed. More than that, I was devastated. I'd talked myself into the test being positive and us being parents. I thought it was the answer to my problem.'

'Your problem? What was that?' Scarlett cut a piece of chicken and chewed it while waiting for Noah's reply. Scarlett couldn't imagine how a baby would have helped Noah at that time.

'I knew I was falling in love with you.' Noah's voice was soft and his eyes held an ocean of love. Scarlett couldn't believe what she was hearing. 'I also thought it would be a disaster for you if we did get together as I believed at that time that I would let down everyone who relied on me. That was why I didn't let people get close. I was protecting them. Or so I thought.'

'And now?' Scarlett watched him as he thought about his answer. He'd been falling in love with her. That caused a melting feeling inside her. She longed to hear him say he loved her.

'I feel as if a weight has been lifted as you'd expect. But...'

Scarlett waited. As a psychiatric nurse she knew that you had to give people the space to answer a question and not jump in with unnecessary comments or unwanted suggestions. So she waited.

His face in the light from the candelabra on the table was a mixture of shadows, dips and hollows. His hair looked almost black.

He sighed. 'I've come to realise that I'm still capable of letting people down. I let you down when I didn't stay to talk through the negative pregnancy test. I thought you were glad it was negative, which hurt me even more. I was confused by the way I felt. I wanted that test to be positive but I wanted you to feel the same way. If I'd stayed instead of being selfish and a coward, we could have discussed it. I'm really sorry.'

They ate their meal, which was delicious. Scarlett glanced at Noah, thoughtfully chewing his steak.

'How long have you been feeling like this? Wanting to be a father I mean?' Scarlett wasn't convinced that Noah still wanted her and not just the baby. They were being honest with each other, possibly for the first time.

'I don't know. That's the truth. I've put up barriers since Dom died, but once I got to know you, they started to come down, little by little. I think it all began at your birthday party.'

'The preposterous comment?' Scarlett cringed. She didn't think she was ever going to live that down.

Noah grinned. 'Exactly. I should have been glad you had no feelings for me. It meant we could be work colleagues and friends with no risk of other feelings muddying the waters. But I didn't feel glad. I was hurt and my fragile male pride had been well and truly dented. No man wants to think a gorgeous woman fancying him is preposterous.'

'I was drunk, I didn't mean it.' She finished her chicken and sat back in her seat.

'I remember,' Noah said with a gentle smile.

'Seeing as how we're being honest, I'll tell you the real reason. My friend, Megs, asked me if I thought she had a chance with you. I panicked. I didn't want her to have you, but I didn't want her to think I wanted you. Not then. My feelings were all over the place. I never meant to upset you. I'm sorry.'

'You're forgiven.'

Noah was feeling content. He was enjoying a good meal with the woman he loved. They were talking honestly in a way they never had before. He was conscious of the fact that they hadn't said those three little words to each other yet but was confident that it was only a matter of time.

The waiter brought the dessert menu. They ordered pannacotta and a latte each, and then Scarlett asked, 'Noah? Tell me honestly. Miranda. Did you fancy her at all? Because she fancied you. Even a teeny tiny bit? Please be honest. I won't hold it against you.'

He had always known that Miranda had been an issue for Scarlett and he needed to reassure her once and for all. He leaned forward and took her hands. 'I promise that I have never fancied Miranda, not even a teeny tiny weeny whiny bit.'

Scarlett laughed which was the response he was looking for.

'Okay. I believe you, even though you took her to Pizza First and gave her the money to pay the deposit and rent.'

'Who told you that?'

'Miranda. Who else?'

'I was trying to help. Anyway, you get on well with Miranda now don't you?'

'Yes, now that Miranda and Ashley are an item I get on better with her. But Ashley's asked her to move in with him so we're back to square one.'

This was his chance. He could ask her to live with him. But was it too soon? 'What are you going to do?'

'Live at Mum's and rent our house out.'

'And is Maria okay with that?'

'Oh yes, Maria is delighted. She loves living at home. I don't think she ever wanted to leave, but she did it to help Esme and myself. That's the kind of person she is.'

'And you? How do you feel about living back at home?'

'We're lucky that Mum's willing to have us back.'

'That wasn't what I asked.'

He watched her expression and saw a spirit of determination in her eyes. She was challenging him. To do what? Man up and take responsibility? Tell her he loved her?

'Well, Noah, that rather depends on you.'

'In what way?'

'You need to find somewhere else to live. We're going to have a baby together.' She waited for him to bring the thought to its logical conclusion. Noah obliged.

'I never dreamed in my wildest moments that I'd ever be in this situation. To be in love with a woman as gorgeous as you and going to be a father. I love you so much, Scarlett and I want us to be a family in our own home. Just the three of us.'

'Thank you for saying it first. I love you too, Noah, and I want the same. A place that we can truly be a family.' Scarlett's eyes shone with an inner light, and her smile was wide and open.

'And this time, we are definitely on the same page.' They held hands and kissed.

CHAPTER THIRTY

C eline sat in the armchair, looking the picture of health. She had dressed up for their appointment, wearing a long, flowing dress with a turban in the same material, both covered in sequins and beads that sparkled like jewels. Her make-up was expertly applied and her eyes were clear and twinkled in the light.

'You're looking well, Celine. How have you been?'

'I'm feeling well, Noah. In fact, I'm feeling better than I've done for years, all thanks to you.'

'Did you contact the people on the list I gave you?'

'I certainly did. I go to meetings twice a week and there's a man who is my buddy and is always on the end of the phone if I think I'm going to drink. He talks me down and sometimes comes to see me. He hasn't had a drink for nearly thirty years. He's an inspiration.'

'That's great. Sounds as if you don't need me anymore.'

'I think I'll always need you, Noah. You've been the one constant in this whole thing. Just knowing you were there at the end of the phone when I needed you has made such a difference.'

'I'm glad. I'll always be at the end of the phone, that will never change.'

'Thank you from the bottom of my heart. I'm hoping I'll need fewer appointments as time goes on, but I'll never forget what you've done for me. And guess what?'

'What?' Noah loved hearing good news from his patients. It made it all worthwhile.

'I've started a vlog—which is like a blog but by video—I tell my followers about my journey and give them as much advice and encouragement as I can. I invite them to comment and I've got thousands of followers already.'

'That's fantastic, Celine.' Her excitement was infectious and Noah couldn't help grinning. 'Well done. I'm so proud of you.'

'Oh, Noah, that's so sweet. But I want to know what has happened in your life. You look so different. You're smiling, not frowning. You look more relaxed. Are you in love?'

Noah—the old Noah—would have clammed up and changed the subject quickly. But the new Noah wanted to share his happiness with the world, even his patients.

'Yes, I am in love and we're having a baby.'

Then he did something he would never have allowed to happen before. When Celine stood up with her arms outstretched for a hug, he let her wrap her arms around him and he hugged her back. It was comforting and empowering and, in that brief moment, they were both happy and knew they deserved to be.

CHAPTER THIRTY-ONE

Noah walked around with a huge grin on his face. From rock bottom he now had his head in the clouds and found concentrating on anything but Scarlett, their baby and their future extremely difficult. He couldn't believe that Scarlett had felt the same way as he did and neither of them were able to articulate it.

Esme had summed it up; all it took was a conversation. People so rarely talked enough about the things that mattered. From now on, he would let Scarlett know how he was feeling and talk through any problems, real or imagined.

One practical thing he needed to turn his attention to was finding them somewhere to live. With him still staying at Joel and Esme's and Scarlett with her mum and sisters, the physical side of their relationship was almost non-existent. They needed a place of their own.

He signed on with the local estate agents and agreed with Scarlett that they'd go house hunting the following Saturday.

'I arranged for us to see four today, all different so we can pin down what we both want in our home,' he said as he drove them to the first viewing. 'The descriptions are in the glove compartment if you want to take a look.'

'Great,' said Scarlett as she read the details of each.

The first was a newbuild. A four bedroomed detached. It was a beautiful house and being brand new, everything was pristine. It was in an area with other houses that looked the same. Maybe Scarlett would think the houses were too regimented. But it turned out she didn't like it for a different reason.

'What do you think?' Noah asked after they had done the tour.

'There's no garden.'

'Is that a deal breaker? A garden?'

'Yes. I'm really into gardening. Since Esme showed me how to do it, I love it. It's so rewarding. We should have a garden. Especially for our child.'

'Okay. Shall we look at the rest of it in case we can find a similar house with a garden?'

'If you like.'

Scarlett didn't like the house, that was obvious. 'What is it you don't like, Scarlett? Just for the record.'

'It would be fine for someone who wanted a show home, but it's too perfect for me. Pristine, shiny, chrome everywhere. I'd be scared to touch anything. I want a house that's been lived in and loved. Somewhere we can relax. A place we can call home.'

'Right. Point taken. No new build then. Let's get to the next one.'

The second house was a semi-detached Edwardian house. Four bedrooms and a garden this time. One that needed a lot of work.

'What do you think?' asked Noah, 'It's got a garden.'

'Yep. The hallway's narrow and it looked a bit dark to me. Sorry, not getting the feels.'

'No feels. Right. Number three then.'

The third house was a nineteen fifties detached, again with four bedrooms.

'I really like this one,' said Noah once they'd seen it all. 'It's got a lovely garden, three reception rooms, and an open-plan kitchen/diner. Do you like it Scarlett?'

'It does have a lovely garden, I'll give you that, but we don't need three reception rooms and all they've done is put a wall up and called it a room.'

'We can always knock that wall down.'

'That is true. It would make the layout a bit strange though,' Scarlett said thoughtfully.

'Could we put it down as a possible? I rather like it.'

'Okay, if you like. But before we see the last one let's get some lunch and have a sit down. We can talk about it.'

'Great idea. We'll have a pub lunch and a rest.'

Noah was happy despite Scarlett not liking any of the houses. Just being in her company, looking at places that could, potentially, become their family home was an amazing experience. He never thought he'd be in this position, planning a future with the woman he loved. He was determined to make every second count. And it could take some time to find the perfect house that they both liked. He had the feeling that when they saw it, they'd know.

He went to the bar and ordered two scampi and chips and two lemon and limes. He glanced over at where Scarlett sat, watching him. She smiled at him and his heart swelled with love. It was the three of them from now on, together forever.

Scarlett couldn't help watching Noah. She couldn't take her eyes off him. It was as if she was dreaming. She loved him so much and couldn't believe he felt the same way. She'd loved him before he found out the truth of Dom's death. But since he'd been told it hadn't been his fault, he'd been a different man. Light-hearted, cheerful, more relaxed and much happier.

He came back with the drinks and sat as close to her as he could. 'Cheers,' he said touching his glass to hers.

'Cheers,' she replied.

'How do you feel about not being able to drink?' he asked.

'Fine. I've given alcohol up. Even when the baby's born, I'm going to be teetotal.'

'Why?'

'Because you're not drinking so neither am I. It'll make life easier.'

'Will you drink when you're with other people?'

'No. I'm giving it up completely. It won't be hard. No more hangovers and we'll save a fortune if we're not buying booze. Lemonade doesn't cost much. I might start making my own.'

'I can't believe you're doing this for me.' Noah's voice was husky and he gave her a misty-eyed look.

'I'll do anything for you. I love you, Noah.' Scarlett loved the fact that she could tell him she loved him. She now knew what it was to be in love. Not roses around the door, or cupids flying around, but proper grown-up love. Planning the future together. Looking for a home. Having a family.

'And I love you and I feel humble that you'd do this. Thank you.'

They kissed just as the waitress brought their food.

When the lunch was over, Noah looked at the description of house number four.

'I'm not sure it's worth bothering about this one said Noah. "The accommodation is ripe for improvement or extension," which is estate agent speak for it needs a lot of work doing to it.'

'Is there a garden?'

'Yes, quite a large one with mature trees beyond the end of the garden, so it won't be overlooked.'

'Oh, it sounds perfect—let's go and see.'

Scarlett felt excited at the thought of the house. She rather fancied the idea of a house they could work on themselves. Put their own stamp on it. A doer upper. Their first home together.

The house was empty and looked neglected and sad. But Scarlett didn't see it as it was, she saw the house it would be when they'd finished renovating it.

The agent stayed downstairs talking on his mobile while they looked at the other floors. The old-fashioned carpets looked torn and threadbare, the kitchen had a cooker and a fridge but little else. The attic had a floor and windows but needed a lot more doing to it before it was habitable.

'Look at that view,' said Scarlett as she gazed down the length of the garden to the trees and the field beyond. 'It's beautiful from up here, don't you think?'

'You want this house, don't you, Scarlett?'

'Yes. I want us to work on this house together. To turn it into our family home. I could be happy here, I know it.'

'It's going to need a lot of work. And with the baby on the way…' Noah sounded unsure but Scarlett wanted the house.

'It doesn't matter how long it takes to do it up. We'll have fun working on it. A bit like people really. We constantly need to work on ourselves to be the people we know we can be. The house is the same.'

'That was profound.' Noah took her in his arms and she felt a deep sense of peace. She hugged him and put her head on his chest. His heartbeat was strong and steady.

'If you're happy, my darling, then I'm happy. I'd live in a tent so long as you were with me. There's just one more thing before we put an offer in. I want to do this in the place we'll live together, have children and grow old.'

'What's that?' Scarlett was hardly listening, she was too happy in his arms, her eyes shut tightly.

Noah gently put her away from him, then fell to one knee and took a small square box out of his pocket. Scarlett held her breath. Was he going to…? The world stood still and everything in it held its breath as Noah looked up at her with a look of love so complete that the tears collected behind her eyes. Happy tears.

'I love you, Scarlett, and I wish I could express the way I feel. But I can't so I'll simply ask—Will you marry me?'

Scarlett's tears fell but she ignored them. 'Yes—oh yes!'

Noah laughed and she helped him to his feet. He slipped the ring on her finger. A diamond solitaire that fitted perfectly.

They kissed and the world began turning again.

He held her as they both gazed out of the window.

'I'm so happy, Noah. I never dreamed that I could ever feel this way.'

'Me too.'

She turned in his arms and they kissed.

The agent came up the stairs and was just about to say something when he saw the couple together. He smiled and quietly made his way back down the stairs.

Also By

Sign up for my newsletter and get Roses for his Rival Free.
Just click https://jburrowsauthor.com/

Letter from the Author

Thank you for reading From the Heart. I hope you enjoyed Scarlett and Noah's story and took them to *your* hearts.

As I was writing this book, I realised how similar some of the story was to Book One. Both Esme and Noah were feeling guilty about causing the death of someone they were close to. And both were leading "lesser" lives as a consequence. In order for them to be free of their chains, they fell in love, let that person into their hearts and allowed the healing process to start.

One of the reasons I love writing romance stories is because I really do believe that love conquers all. The opposite of love isn't hate as some people think, it is fear. Both Esme and Noah were living in fear. It took sweet-natured Joel and spirited Scarlett to break down the barriers and allow their soulmates to live life to the full again.

There are two more books in this series and I can't wait to introduce them to you. Maria is a carer in a residential care home; Connie is now a qualified nurse. They are totally different characters to their sisters so their stories will be very different. I'm hoping to publish both these books by the end of 2023.

One more thing… if you enjoyed From the Heart, I'd be grateful if you would be willing to write a review. It doesn't have to be long – one sentence will do. Or just a ranking. The more reviews a book gets the higher it will rise in the Amazon rankings. And more importantly, it will bring the book to the attention of more readers.

I'll end by thanking you again for reading this book. I am grateful for every reader and will endeavour to bring you more love stories with happy ever afters and characters to fall in love with!

With love,

Jax

Printed in Great Britain
by Amazon